He knew he had no choice but to help her.

"Come on," Cade said roughly. "Let's get out of here."

Piper frowned. "Where are we going? Back to my car?"

"No. My ranch isn't far from here. It'll be safer there. We can figure out what to do next."

"'We?'" she echoed faintly. "Why would you want to help me?"

It was a good question, one he would have asked if he was in her shoes, one he was still asking himself.

A smart man would get away from this woman and her mess as fast as humanly possible. But it seemed he wasn't that smart.

So, he gave the only answer he could. "Because somebody needs to."

KERRY CONNOR

HER COWBOY DEFENDER

TORONTO NEW YORK LONDON
AMSTERDAM PARIS SYDNEY HAMBURG
STOCKHOLM ATHENS TOKYO MILAN MADRID
PRAGUE WARSAW BUDAPEST AUCKLAND

To Jodi, who introduced me to New Mexico,
for being the kind of friend who's there when I need her,
even when she's on the other side of the world.

Recycling programs
for this product may
not exist in your area.

ISBN-13: 978-0-373-74655-2

HER COWBOY DEFENDER

Copyright © 2012 by Kerry Connor

www.Harlequin.com

Printed in U.S.A.

ABOUT THE AUTHOR

A lifelong mystery reader, Kerry Connor first discovered romance suspense by reading Harlequin Intrigue books and is thrilled to be writing for the line. Kerry lives and writes in New York.

Books by Kerry Connor

HARLEQUIN INTRIGUE

Don't miss any of our special offers. Write to us at the following address for information on our newest releases.

Harlequin Reader Service
U.S.: 3010 Walden Ave., P.O. Box 1325, Buffalo, NY 14269
Canadian: P.O. Box 609, Fort Erie, Ont. L2A 5X3

CAST OF CHARACTERS

Piper Lowry—On a desperate mission to save her sister, she finds an unexpected defender in the form of a long, tall cowboy.

Cade McClain—The rancher's honor demands that he offer his help, even if it means risking everything for a stranger.

Esteban Castillo—A man who wants information...and vengeance.

Matt Alvarez—Cade's right-hand man warns him not to get involved—for more than one reason.

Pamela Lowry—Piper's twin sister is in a coma.

Tara Lowry—Piper's younger sister is a pawn in a dangerous game.

Jay Larson—He's on Piper's trail, but what are his true motives?

Chapter One

This can't be happening.

Piper stared in disbelief at the black smoke billowing from the engine of the rental car. She'd barely managed to pull over to the side of the road before the giant plume erupted from beneath the hood, along with a crackling she suspected might be outright fire. Any hope the car would keep running long enough to make it to her destination evaporated into the air much faster than the smoke.

She shot a glance at the clock on the dashboard. The digits glared back, relentless, unforgiving.

Thirty-four minutes. She had thirty-four minutes to be at the rendezvous point. If she wasn't—

No.

She cut off the thought before it could form. She couldn't afford to think about that, couldn't think about anything but what she was going to do now, how she was going to make the deadline.

But when she tried to come up with a solution to this latest hurdle, her mind remained stubbornly blank except for the words that had been running through her head nonstop for the past two days.

This can't be happening.

The words raced together in a constant loop, picking up speed along with her pulse, her heart pounding so fast and so hard in her chest she found it tougher and tougher to breathe.

It couldn't end like this. She couldn't come this close only to fail.

This can't be happening.

Beneath the shock clouding her brain, some preservation instinct forced her limbs into motion, recognizing the fact that it wasn't safe to remain in the car. For all she knew, the engine could explode at any moment. She had to get out of there.

Numbly, she switched off the key, then grabbed her bag and the map. Lurching from the vehicle, she slammed the door shut behind her. It was all she could do not to give the door an angry kick. She'd known as soon as she heard the knocking sound that something was wrong, but couldn't stop. Even if time wasn't an issue, she knew nothing about cars. She had no choice but to keep pushing on and hope she made it to her destination.

So much for that.

Which just left what she was going to do now.

The sun beat down from directly overhead, her fair skin already beginning to tingle under the unrelenting beams. Raising a hand to shade her eyes, she glanced around. The desert road stretched endlessly in either direction, disappearing into the horizon on both sides with no indication where it stopped. She had no idea where she was, other than that it was somewhere in New Mexico. She'd been following the map that had been provided to her, having no other choice. She hadn't passed a single vehicle or building on the road in at least a half hour, had no reason to believe she would find any the same distance up ahead if she started walking. She'd known that she was being sent to the middle of nowhere, but she was more aware of that fact now than ever before.

She checked her watch, already knowing what it would show, painfully aware of how quickly time was slipping away.

Thirty-two minutes.

The backs of her eyes began to burn, and she immediately squeezed her eyelids together to keep the tears that threatened from falling. She wasn't going to cry. She refused to. She hadn't one bit since this ordeal had begun. She hadn't cried when she'd learned of Pam's accident. She hadn't cried when she'd received the horrible call two days ago. She hadn't cried during the long journey, even knowing what awaited her at the end.

But never had she been as close to giving in to the tears as she was right now.

A sob rose in her throat.

This can't be happening.

With her eyes shut, it was the sound of an engine that reached her first, the sound so faint she didn't immediately recognize it. When she did, she froze in disbelief, afraid to open her eyes, afraid she was hallucinating. It seemed too much to hope for, too much to believe possible, that a vehicle could pass by at this particular moment when she needed it most.

Her heart pounding anew, she slowly opened her eyes and turned toward the sound.

The vehicle was still far enough away that she could barely make it out, its shape shimmering in the sun, almost like a mirage. She held her breath as it approached, gradually gaining enough substance to confirm that it was very real. It was a pickup truck. Red, she guessed, though it hardly mattered. All that did was that it was here.

The black cloud rising from the hood made her car pretty hard to ignore, but she still stepped out into the road, waving her arms above her head to grab the driver's attention. She couldn't risk that the driver was the kind of person to ignore someone in trouble. A breath of relief worked its way from her lungs when the truck began to slow long before it reached her, easing onto the shoulder behind the rental car.

Now she just had to figure out what to do.

Thinking quickly, she watched as the driver's door slowly opened. Moments later, two boots hit the dirt beneath the bottom edge of the door, one after the other. Then a hat appeared as the driver ducked his head out of the truck. It was a Stetson, the shape unmistakable and instantly recognizable.

It was a cowboy. A genuine cowboy. A near-hysterical laugh bubbled in her throat. She didn't exactly come across too many of them back in Boston, though they were probably fairly common around these parts. And here he was, coming to her rescue like something out of the Old West, except that instead of on horseback, he was arriving in a truck.

A truck.

Her eyes slid past him, narrowing on his vehicle, the burst of humor instantly forgotten.

Cold, hard resolve settled over her, and she slowly lowered her hand into her bag, closing her fingers around the object there.

And suddenly she knew exactly what she had to do.

CADE MCCLAIN SWALLOWED AN impatient sigh as he climbed out of the cab of the truck. He really didn't have time for this. The trip to Albuquerque had taken longer than he'd expected, and he'd wanted to get back to the ranch as early as possible. There was too much he had to do. There always was.

But as soon as he'd spotted the smoke on the road up ahead and seen the car, he'd known he would have to pull over. Even if the woman hadn't flagged him down, he couldn't have simply driven past a smoking car without stopping. Not only would it have been a lousy thing to do, but there was no telling when someone else might have come along to help. This desert road didn't see much traffic. He wondered how long she'd been here, or what she was even doing here for that matter.

She'd moved out of the road to stand behind

her car. He gave her a quick once-over. She was a slim woman with black hair that brushed her shoulders, dressed in a T-shirt and jeans. She carried a bag of some kind, the strap slung crosswise over her body from one shoulder to the opposite hip so the bag itself was almost entirely out of view. She didn't look familiar. Probably just a lost tourist who'd made a wrong turn somewhere and ended up far down a road she had no business being on.

He did his best to keep his annoyance from showing. It wasn't her fault she was having car trouble. It had to be a lot tougher on her than it was on him.

"You okay?" he called, stepping around the door without closing it.

After a moment, she gave her head a shaky nod. "Yeah, I'm fine. I don't know what happened. The engine started making this noise, and then all this smoke started coming out of it…."

Her voice quivered, almost like she was about to start crying or something, and he nearly groaned.

Oh, God. Please don't let her burst into tears. The car he might be able to handle, but the last thing he knew how to deal with was a crying female.

He took a deep breath, hoping if he remained calm his coolness would have an effect on her. "Do you have a phone? Did you call anybody?"

"N-no," she said slowly, taking a step toward him. "My battery's dead." She chuckled, the sound ringing false. "Just my luck."

"Well, you can borrow mine. Let me get it out of the cab." He turned away to do just that.

"I have a better idea."

Her tone immediately put him on edge, the hardness in her voice completely different from how she'd sounded just moments before. He froze, knowing before he looked at her that something was wrong.

He slowly turned back to face her.

She was standing in exactly the same place.

Except now she held a pistol in her hands.

Aimed square at his chest.

Chapter Two

"Throw your keys on the ground in front of my feet," she ordered. "Don't try anything tricky."

Cade did his best to ignore the gun, meeting the eyes behind it. Only now did he recognize the desperation in her voice. Earlier he'd mistaken it for the understandable distress of a woman whose car had caught fire in the middle of nowhere. But this went way beyond that. The woman was seriously on edge.

That still didn't make her actions any more comprehensible.

"What the hell do you think you're doing?" he demanded.

"Taking your truck."

"It's not much. Certainly not worth stealing."

"It runs, which is more than I can say for that car. That's all that matters."

"And you're just going to leave me out here in the middle of nowhere? No water? No shelter?

Nothing to do but hope somebody else comes along?"

"I'm sorry about this. I really am. But I have to be somewhere in less than thirty minutes, and it really is a matter of life and death. I know how clichéd that sounds, but in this case, it couldn't be more true. Now toss your keys over toward me."

He didn't move, the weight of his keys suddenly heavy in his fingers. He quickly considered his few options. Maybe if he pretended to throw them, distracted her long enough to dive back into the truck—

She cocked the weapon, her expression hard as stone.

"I told you, don't even think of trying anything. If you don't think it's worth stealing, then it's certainly not worth getting shot over."

"But it is worth shooting somebody for?"

"If I have to."

He stared at her, gauging her seriousness.

The way she handled the gun, her grip tight and unwavering, told him she knew exactly how to use it.

The way she looked at him, her eyes cold and unflinching, told him she wouldn't hesitate to.

Damn. It didn't look like he had a choice.

Biting back a curse, he slowly swung his arm

and tossed the keys toward her. He didn't bother to see where they landed.

She flicked her gaze down for only a second, not nearly long enough for him to make a move if he was crazy enough to try. When her attention was back on his face, she bent slowly at the knees, never losing her aim on him. As soon as she was close enough to the ground, she lowered one hand from the gun just long enough to scoop up the keys which had landed practically at her feet. As soon as she had them, she immediately started to rise again, gesturing toward him with a jerk of her chin. "Step away."

He did as ordered, slowly moving backward, one frustrating step following another. After his first few steps, she was again on her feet and began to match his motions, stepping forward to the truck. Finally he was standing well behind the tailgate and she came to a stop next to the still-open door.

She glanced inside, then began to climb into the truck. Her movements were awkward, since she was still keeping the gun on him with one hand, but her aim remained true enough. "I really am sorry about this," she said. "I'll toss your phone out the window on the other side. You can call someone to come and get you."

"You aren't worried we'll catch up with you?"

"By the time you do, it won't matter anymore," she said flatly.

Before he could wonder what she meant by that, she started to straighten in the seat, only to stop. A second later, she glanced back at him. "This is a manual."

"Yeah, so?"

"I can't drive a stick shift."

He snorted. "Well, that's too bad for you."

She didn't say anything for a moment, staring at him long and hard. "You're going to have to drive."

"Excuse me?"

She jerked her head toward the cab. "Get in."

An incredulous laugh burst from his mouth. "You've gotta be kidding me. It's not enough you want to steal my truck. Now you want to hijack me into being your driver?"

"I don't have a choice. The way I see it, neither do you."

"Or what? You're going to shoot me? Then who's going to drive you?"

"If you refuse to drive me, then I'm not going to be where I need to be in time and somebody very important to me is going to die. So I might as well shoot you, because you will have just killed someone I love."

The seriousness in her voice killed the last

traces of dark humor inside him. He hadn't considered her earlier words too deeply, but the intensity in this statement left no doubt she meant everything she said. Something was going on here. Someone she cared about was in very real danger. She believed that much.

Still, Cade hesitated. If anything, her words gave him more of a reason to want out of this. Whatever this mess was, it wasn't something any sane person would want any part of.

She motioned with the gun. "If you think I won't do it, I sincerely suggest you think again."

And he saw the truth in her eyes. She would shoot him without a second thought. If he wanted to keep breathing, his only chance was to go along with her demand. And as much as he didn't want to be killed, he didn't really want to be responsible for it happening to someone else, either.

Matching her glare, he started forward slowly. After a few moments, she disappeared inside the cab. When he reached the open door, he found she'd slid across the seat and was backed up against the passenger door. The gun in her hands instantly adjusted so the barrel was centered right on his head.

Climbing in, he glanced down to find the keys already in the ignition. No point delaying the obvious, he supposed. With a grimace, he tugged the door shut, then reached forward and started the engine.

"All right," he said, shifting the truck into gear. "Where are we going?"

HOLDING THE GUN STEADY with her right hand, Piper pulled the map from her bag and held it out to him. "Here."

He took it from her with some reluctance, giving it a perfunctory glance. "What is this?"

"Where I need to go."

He looked at it again, frowning slightly. "This is Cartwright."

"What's that?"

"An old ghost town in the middle of the desert. There's not much there now."

"Well, there will be in twenty-five minutes." At the very least *someone*. Several someones most likely, but there was only one she truly cared about being there. "If you know where it is, then you must know how to get there."

"Yeah."

"Then drive."

Clenching the map in his hand, he pulled back onto the road and started forward.

"Can we get there in twenty-five minutes?" she asked.

"Probably."

"That isn't good enough. Drive fast—but not fast enough that anything bad should happen. Neither of us wants this gun to go off accidentally."

The muscles on his neck bulged from his clear tension, but he didn't respond. The truck accelerated smoothly, picking up speed without jostling her.

She kept her eyes on him, not about to let her guard down when so much depended on him cooperating and getting her where she needed to be. He stared straight ahead, his jaw clenched. It was a strong jaw, perfectly fitting his plainly masculine profile. He had to be in his late thirties, his skin tanned from the sun, faint laugh lines worn into the corners around his eyes. It was a nice face. She suspected he was a nice guy. She remembered the clear thread of concern in his deep voice when he'd first pulled over. All he'd wanted to do was help her. And she'd pointed a gun at him and threatened to kill him.

Guilt, sharp and painful, stabbed at her. She ruthlessly pushed the feeling aside. The people she was dealing with weren't letting anything stop them from getting what they wanted. She couldn't afford to, either. And given a choice between Tara and this stranger, there was no question what she would do. The only thing that mattered was getting to the rendezvous on time, whatever it took.

Then it hit her. No, that wasn't all that mattered. What happened at the meeting also mattered a great deal. She'd had a plan, a risky, dangerous, improbable plan, but the only one—the only chance—she had. The rental car had been a key part of that plan. Without it, this wasn't going to work.

Unless…

She sharpened her gaze on the man behind the wheel, studying that hardened face. He'd wanted to help her once. He must be a good person, or at least good enough for what she needed him to do.

"I need to ask you a favor," she said.

"Lady, you're holding a gun on me. You're not asking, you're ordering."

"Not with this. This is for when I'm gone and don't have the gun on you anymore. I need you to do something for me then."

"Why the hell would I do anything else for you, lady?"

"Because I'm hoping that the kind of guy who couldn't drive by and leave a woman standing on the side of the road won't leave an innocent woman in danger, either."

He snorted. "I hate to break it to you, but you're kidding yourself if you think you're innocent."

"I'm not talking about me. My sister's been kidnapped. We're making the exchange at this location. I'm not going to give them what they want until my sister is safely out of there. My original plan was for her to drive away, but obviously that's not an option anymore. So I need to ask you to please stay long enough to get her out of there."

"What about you?"

"Don't worry about me. She's all that matters."

His frown deepened. "Who are these people? Why did they kidnap your sister?"

"That's not important."

"The hell it's not. If you want me to stick around these people, I need to know what I'm up against."

"They kidnapped her to force…me to provide them…with some information they want."

"Even if they let your sister go before you give it to them, what do you think they're going to do to you after you give it to them?"

"I told you, don't worry about me."

"It sounds like somebody needs to. What's going to happen to you after you give them what they want?"

"Her name is Tara," she said as if he hadn't spoken. "She's only twenty years old. She has her whole life ahead of her."

"And you don't? You can't be much older than thirty, if that. What about your life?"

"*Please.* I know I don't have the right to ask you for anything, but I'm doing it anyway. Please save my sister. If you want me to beg, if that's what it will take to get you to agree, then I will do it. It should be clear by now that I am willing to do anything to save her. So I'm asking you, begging you, *please* save my sister."

Something in his face softened slightly, and hope burst in her chest at the indication that she might have swayed him.

He never had a chance to answer.

The rear window suddenly shattered. Glass sprayed into the interior of the truck. Piper cringed, instinctively turning away from the blast. Almost immediately, she whipped her head back to see what had happened.

A car had pulled up behind them without her noticing. She hadn't been paying close enough attention while she'd been speaking to him, hadn't even considered that she would need to.

Then she saw the arm reaching out of the driver's side window, the glint of a gun clutched in a hand, just before a dull thud struck the metal of the truck.

Realization struck as hard as the impact of a bullet. Someone was shooting at them, trying to force them off the road before she could even get to the rendezvous point.

Oh, God.

She should have known they wouldn't play fair.

Chapter Three

The sound of another bullet hitting metal knocked Piper out of the shock holding her in place.

The driver of the other car wasn't the only one with a gun.

Gritting her teeth, she turned all the way around in her seat, just as the cowboy shouted, "Friends of yours?"

"Just keep driving!" she yelled, pushing her arms out the shattered back window and taking aim. As soon as she had her target, she pulled the trigger.

She didn't hear anything, but the shot must have hit, because the car wavered slightly, sliding across the road. Satisfaction surged inside her, but she never let the vehicle out of her sights, matching her movements to it.

Confident she had another shot, she took it.

The windshield cracked.

She shot twice more in quick succession.

The glass cracked farther, the webbing spreading across the windshield. If she wasn't mistaken, there was no way the driver should be able to see through it.

As if to confirm it, the car suddenly skidded across the road. Seconds later, it went right over the edge of the shoulder, disappearing from view.

A triumphant grin briefly flashed across her lips, the feeling unfamiliar, before she sobered, pulling her arms back into the truck and turning to the cowboy.

"I guess you really do know how to use that," he said drily.

"And don't forget it."

He didn't reply, frowning slightly. She watched his eyes lower to the panel in front of him. It was only then she realized they were gradually losing speed.

"Why are you slowing down?"

"Something's wrong."

She cocked the gun. "Knock it off. We don't have time for this."

"I'm not doing anything," he snapped. "I think he got one of the tires."

"He couldn't have. The tire would have blown."

"Then something must have ricocheted into it or we hit something."

Dread shot through her. "Ignore it. Keep going."

"I can't ignore it. The truck isn't going to let me."

"How much farther do we have to go?"

"Too far. We'll never make it."

Before she could argue further, he was already easing off the accelerator and pulling over onto the shoulder.

She opened her mouth to tell him once more to keep going, but even as she did, she could feel the truck was starting to list on its left rear tire.

The cowboy shifted the truck into Park and shut off the engine, then opened his door and stepped out without even acknowledging her. Piper quickly scrambled across the seat and followed.

To her horror, the tire was already half-deflated. It must have been a graze or a nick or something, since the tire hadn't exploded, though it might as well have for what the damage meant.

They didn't have time for this. "Change the tire," she ordered.

"I'm going to," he grumbled. "It's the only way I can get out of here."

"How long is it going to take?"

"Long enough."

"I only have fifteen minutes!"

He finally glanced back at her. This time there was a trace of sympathy in his eyes that shook her more than anything he could say. "I'm sorry," he said softly. "I don't think you're going to make it."

She raised the gun at him. "Not good enough."

He simply shook his head and turned away. "You can shoot me, but it won't change anything."

She didn't want to believe him. She wanted to scream, call him a liar.

But as she watched him work, she realized with a sinking heart that he was right. Changing a tire on a pickup truck was a bigger task than on a passenger car. He didn't seem to be taking his time, but it was still taking far too long. And even if he managed to get the tire changed quickly, they still had to travel to their destination.

She peered down the road, raising a hand to her face to shade her eyes. There was nothing but the strip of highway and endless stretches of desert as far as the eye could see. No indication that they were anywhere near where she needed to be.

Finding it suddenly hard to breathe, she

pulled the cell phone out of her bag with one hand, even though there wasn't much of a point. She couldn't even call the kidnapper to beg for more time. The two times she'd spoken with him, he'd called her from an unlisted number. All the contact came from his end. She had no way of reaching him.

All she could do was stand there, feeling time—and Tara's life—slipping away from her with each passing moment.

She watched in horror as her watch counted down to the appointed meeting time all too quickly, then reached it.

No.

She stood frozen, waiting for something to happen. Something *should* happen. The end of her world, the end of her sister's life, couldn't just pass like this, uneventful, in silence.

At exactly two minutes past, the cell phone suddenly rang. She glanced at the screen even though there was no one else it could possibly be. As expected, the caller was identified only as "Unlisted Number."

She quickly took the call. "Hello?"

A long silence echoed across the line before the silky, superior voice she expected finally spoke.

"It would seem I overestimated how much your sister means to you, Ms. Lowry."

"I would have been there if your people hadn't tried to force me off the road! What were you trying to do, get the drive without having to release my sister? We had a deal!"

She'd responded without thinking, the panic and anger inside her too fierce to hold back in the face of the man's condescension and everything that had just happened. She fell silent just as quickly, a fresh wave of panic washing over her. She couldn't afford to make him angry, not if there was any chance left of getting Tara back, not when he held all the cards.

His silence lasted for a torturous eternity.

"I assure you, Ms. Lowry, no one who works for me tried to force you off the road. It's like you said. We have a deal. I wouldn't jeopardize that with foolish tactics that could prevent me from getting what I want."

Of course he was right. If she'd been thinking clearly she would have realized that. "Then who—"

"It would seem that someone doesn't want you to give me the information."

It was on the tip of her tongue to ask who that was, but that was exactly what she couldn't do.

"So what happens now?" she made herself ask calmly instead.

Another silence. She almost wondered if the bastard was really considering his answers this carefully or if he simply enjoyed tormenting her by dragging them out.

"We will have to arrange another meeting," he said finally. "I will be in touch—"

"But Tara—"

"Your sister is fine for the time being," he interrupted with a trace of impatience. "And will remain so as long as you do as you are told."

"How do I know you're telling me the truth? How do I know you didn't try to get to me because my sister is already dead and you didn't have anything to exchange?"

"I suppose you have no choice but to trust me."

"Not good enough—"

"You will be allowed to speak with her when we set up the meeting."

"No, I want to talk to her now—"

He'd already disconnected the call.

A sob rose in her throat, and she nearly gagged holding it back. She couldn't give in to it. If she lost control, she might never get it back again.

The gun was suddenly snatched away from

her, far too quickly for her to tighten the grip she'd unwittingly loosened.

She jerked her head up to find the cowboy standing over her, her gun now clenched in his hand. He didn't point it at her. He simply held it as he stared down at her, his expression thunderous.

"From the sound of your half of that conversation, the immediate danger is over. Now I want to know what the hell is going on."

Chapter Four

Cade knew he was capable of being intimidating. He was a big man, and his sheer size alone was enough to inspire a certain wariness in people at times. He didn't get angry often, certainly not truly angry, but when he did he knew it came across loud and clear. He'd seen more than one ranch hand who'd pulled something over the years cowering in the face of his anger, and after everything this woman had put him through in the past thirty minutes, he was angrier than he'd ever been in his entire life.

The woman didn't even blink. She simply stared up at him, her eyes so bleak and tired he almost felt an involuntary twinge of sympathy before he stifled the feeling.

She gave her head a little shake. "Trust me, you don't want to be involved any more than you already are."

He couldn't argue with her on that. He *didn't* want to be involved in this. But as long as he was, there was no turning back at this point. "So what now, you want me to just leave you here and be on my way?"

"I would appreciate a ride back to my car so I can call for a tow truck, but I'm sure that's too much to ask."

"Yeah, it is, especially since your friend who was shooting at us is back in that direction. You don't think he won't open fire again if he sees us passing by, or he won't try to make his way to you while you're waiting for your tow to show up?"

She frowned, her forehead furrowing, and he could tell she hadn't thought about it at all. "You're right. Then if you could take me to the next town, wherever that is—"

"I'm not going anywhere until I know what's going on."

Alarm flared in her eyes. "But we can't stay here. What if that man passes by while we're just standing around—"

"Then you'd better start talking fast."

She scowled at him, her jaw tightening. He could tell she wanted to argue, but must have read in his expression that it wouldn't do her any good.

Finally she cleared her throat. "My sister Pam is an FBI agent—"

"I thought you said your sister's name is Tara," he said sharply, wondering if she was lying to him already, if she hadn't been all along.

"Tara's my younger sister. Like I said, she's only twenty years old. Pam is my twin sister. She's an FBI agent. Late last year she was assigned to the field office in Dallas."

He suddenly realized he didn't know her name. "What about you? What's your name?"

This time she did blink at him. "Oh. It's Piper. Piper Lowry."

He couldn't have said why, but it suited her. "Okay. Go on."

"Two days ago, I was notified that Pam was in a car accident that left her in a coma. I immediately flew to Dallas from Boston—that's where I live. I went straight to the hospital from the airport. The accident was pretty bad. She's in stable condition, but the doctors have no idea when she might wake up. I didn't really get many details about what happened—her doctor made some reference that there was evidence she was driven off the road, but said I should talk to the police. I went there next. The detective I spoke to confirmed that it looked suspicious and said he'd been in contact with the FBI since Pam was a federal agent. He asked if

I had any idea who might want to harm her. I told him I didn't.

"After that I went to Pam's house. When I got there, the phone rang. I wasn't going to answer it, but when the answering machine picked up, this man—older-sounding, with a slight accent—began speaking. He said they knew I was home and that I'd better stop playing games and pick up the phone if I ever wanted to see my sister alive again.

"I picked up, of course. My first thought was that the man was talking about Pam. I had no idea Tara was missing or in any way involved. The man said he was aware of my accident, which is the only reason he allowed me to miss the original deadline, but he still wanted the information he asked of me."

"He thought you were Pam," Cade concluded.

"Exactly. Obviously I wasn't the sister he was talking about, and we only have one other, so I knew he had to be talking about Tara. I immediately asked if Tara was okay, and he said she was for the time being, but wouldn't be if I didn't have the information he wanted."

"What information?"

"I had no idea. I couldn't tell him that, because then he'd know I wasn't Pam. I was afraid that if he knew she was in a coma and incapable of providing any information, he might decide Tara was no use to him anymore and do something to her. So I said I had it. He told me to check the mailbox. There was an envelope in it with a cell phone they would use to contact me, and he would be in touch with further instructions. He hung up, and I immediately went to the mailbox. The phone was exactly where he said it would be.

"As soon as I got back in the house, I tried to reach Tara. I hadn't spoken to her in a few days, which wasn't unusual. She's in college in Pennsylvania, and is busy with school and everything. I couldn't reach her on her cell, but I did get in touch with her roommate. She said Tara left a few days earlier, leaving a note saying she was heading home for a while because her sister was sick. That would have been before Pam's accident, and nothing had happened to me, so I figured the kidnappers must have left the note so Tara's disappearance wouldn't look suspicious and the police wouldn't be contacted."

"Obviously they contacted Pam once they had Tara," he noted. "She really didn't give you any idea Tara had been kidnapped? Did she try to reach you? What if you tried to call Tara earlier? You would have known the sick-sister story was a lie."

Piper shrugged. "Pam tends to do her own thing and likes to handle matters on her own. She probably thought she could handle the situation herself and get Tara back before I even knew anything had happened. Or else she was so busy dealing with the situation she didn't have time to think about me."

"So did you call the police?"

She shook her head. "I couldn't. I didn't want to do anything to endanger Tara, and I couldn't trust them not to contact the FBI again, which is the protocol in kidnapping cases, especially one involving multiple states, since she was taken in Pennsylvania, not Texas."

"Why didn't you want to contact the FBI? Your sister works for them."

"Exactly. And the information the kidnappers want must be something related to the Dallas field office. Why else would they kidnap the sister of an agent in that office?"

"So wouldn't the FBI be the best people to contact? They would know who would want the information so badly and probably be able to figure out who's behind this and how to stop them."

"Except that's exactly what Pam would have done, and look what happened to her."

He frowned. "What do you mean?"

"Think about it. Who would possibly want to run Pam off the road? The kidnappers wouldn't. They had no reason to. They wouldn't have wanted to endanger her and possibly ruin their chances of getting what they wanted. No, it must have been someone else. The most likely possibility I can come up with is that Pam went to one of her colleagues for help, someone she trusted, and instead of providing it, they tried to stop her from giving the information to the kidnappers."

He gaped at her in disbelief. "You think the FBI would run one of their agents off the road to keep her from releasing classified materials? Wouldn't arresting her be a lot easier?"

"Not the FBI," she said patiently, as though he were the one speaking nonsense. "Someone *within* the FBI who's acting on their own and willing to do whatever it takes to stop this information, whatever it is, from being shared." She sent a nervous glance in the direction they'd come from. "I think what just happened to us proves how desperate this person is."

"What are you talking about?"

"I should have realized it wasn't the kidnappers trying to drive us off the road. I was just so focused on them and trying to get to Tara that, in the heat of the moment, I wasn't thinking straight. But of course it wasn't. It's like the kidnapper said, he wouldn't do anything to jeopardize getting what he wants. It was someone who didn't want me getting to my destination and making delivery to the kidnappers, the same someone who tried to stop Pam from doing the same thing."

Cade tried to think of an explanation for who else might have been shooting at them, but came up empty. She seemed to have thought this all out, not surprising, given that she'd had a lot more time to consider all the possibilities than he had.

Not willing to concede she was right just yet, he decided to set the issue aside for the moment. There was a lot more to this story he needed to hear. "Okay, so you decided not to go to the police or the FBI. What did you do?"

"I tried to figure out what I could do to save Tara and waited for the man to call me back. He finally did last night. He instructed me to drive to Albuquerque and arrive by noon. I left immediately. At noon, he called me with the address of a copy shop where he said a fax would be waiting for me. It was that map that I showed you. I was to be at that location exactly at two."

"What was your plan?"

"I was going to refuse to give them the information until they let Tara go first."

He frowned again. "Did you really think they would agree to that?"

"I wasn't going to give them a choice. I brought a flash drive with me and was going to tell them I would only give them the password to unlock the file on it once they let Tara go."

"Why would they agree to that? They could have just threatened to shoot Tara if you didn't give it to them."

"I was going to throw the flash drive on the ground and say that if they did anything to her I would put a bullet through it and destroy it right then and there. If they tried to shoot me, they would risk me pulling the trigger reflexively and destroying the drive anyway. After going to so much trouble to get the information, I was counting on them not being willing to risk losing it when it was so close at hand. We both had something the other wanted. It would be easier to just make the exchange. And if they threatened to kill her outright, I would have threatened to kill myself if they did, because if anything happened to her, I would have just watched my sister die and wouldn't be able to live with myself if I'd gotten her killed."

"Even if they agreed to let her go, they wouldn't have let you go without the password."

"I know. I was prepared to stay. That was the exchange. Me, the flash drive and the password for Tara."

An uneasy feeling began to churn in his gut. "Do you have the information they want?"

"No. I still don't even know what it is. That's why I had to get them to let Tara go before I agreed to give them the flash drive supposedly containing the information."

"You can't believe they would have agreed to that without knowing you had what they wanted."

"It was the only chance I had, the only chance *Tara* had."

"But once they found out you'd cheated them, they would have killed you."

She stared back at him, unblinking. "I know," she said simply.

He had no response to that, could only stare at her, the magnitude of what she was telling him hitting him square in the chest.

"You can't be serious," he said, unable to hide his disbelief. "What good would that have done? Once they killed you, they would have gone after her to prevent her from talking."

"I was going to try to give her as much time

as I could to get away. I have a map in my bag that I was going to leave in the car with a note telling her to drive to Colorado to get to the police or FBI there and to avoid the main roads. I didn't think they would expect her to go there and would have a harder time tracking her that way. I also didn't think she could trust anyone around here in case the kidnappers had connections with the police or the locals. There had to have been a reason they chose this area for the meeting. Pam had two guns in her house. I had one on me and left the other in the car for Tara. I also had the suitcase I brought with me to Dallas so she would have clothes, though I didn't have time to grab it before I got in your truck. My ATM and credit cards are in my bag, along with enough cash to see her through for a few days. I would have left it in the car for her, too. It was the best I could come up with on the spur of the moment, but I had to pray it would be enough to get her to safety."

Cade studied her, too stunned to do anything else. She really had thought the whole thing through. There was no doubting it. This had been a suicide mission. She'd come here fully expecting to die, and had done so willingly, to save her sister. No, it hadn't just been willing. She'd been desperate to do so, fighting tooth and nail and doing whatever it took to get to a rendezvous where she thought she would die.

She had to understand the enormity of the sacrifice she'd been willing to make. Yet there was no sign of it on her face—no pride, no regret, no misgivings. Just simple straightforwardness, as though it was clear what she'd had to do, as though it were nothing at all.

Maybe it was to her.

He tried to think of anyone he'd ever known who would have been willing to do that for him. Not his father, who'd never wanted a kid in the first place and only cared about what he could find at the bottom of the nearest bottle. Certainly not his mother, who'd walked out on them when he was a boy. Not Caitlin, the one person he thought he would have been willing to do anything for—yeah, probably even die— who'd walked out on him, too. There was Matt Alvarez, his right-hand man on the ranch and the closest thing he had to a friend in this world, but he didn't know if Alvarez would be willing to make such a colossal sacrifice, and frankly, Cade wouldn't expect him to.

He wondered what this sister of hers was like, wondered if she was worthy of the sacrifice this woman had been willing to make. Obviously Piper Lowry thought so.

It suddenly struck him that he was just standing there, staring at the woman in front of him. He cleared his throat, his anger gone, replaced by an emotion he couldn't really name. Any doubts he'd had about her story were gone now. It was far too detailed and she'd related it so unwaveringly she certainly hadn't been making it up on the spot. All that remained was the question of what to do now.

Only one answer came to mind, one he wasn't happy with. But it seemed he didn't have a choice any more than she thought she had.

"Come on," he said roughly. "Let's get out of here."

She frowned. "Where are we going? Back to my car?"

"No. My ranch isn't far from here. It'll be safer there. We can figure out what to do next."

"'We'?" she echoed faintly. "Why would you want to help me?"

It was a good question, one he would have asked if he were in her shoes, one he was still asking himself.

He gave the only answer he could. "Because somebody needs to."

He damn well wished it wasn't him. If he had a brain in his head, it wouldn't be. A smart man would get away from this woman and her mess as fast as humanly possible.

But it seemed he wasn't that smart. And like it or not—and he sure as heck did not—it looked like he was all she had.

Chapter Five

Esteban Castillo stood at the window of the bedroom he'd commandeered as his own and stared out at the vast landscape behind the house. It was a view he'd contemplated often since his arrival, enough that he seemed to have every inch of it committed to memory. When he'd left the house earlier that afternoon, he'd thought he'd seen the last of it. But here he was again, exactly where he'd been before.

This part of the plan should have been completed. He should have the information he needed, be on his way to carrying out the next step, to finishing this matter once and for all. Instead, the vengeance he'd vowed so long ago had been delayed again.

Impatience churned in his gut, the feeling unusual. He was a man who knew the importance of patience. He'd pulled himself out of poverty, built his businesses, made his fortune by knowing how to bide his time when necessary, knowing how to wait, knowing exactly when he should act.

The skill he'd carefully cultivated over the years seemed to be failing him now. But then, this wasn't business. This was very personal.

This was *family*.

The mere thought of the word sent a sharp pain through him; the feeling quickly burned away by the rage that followed closely behind it. He had no family, not anymore. He'd had only one son. He'd certainly never planned it to be that way, but it was the sole instance where his patience was not rewarded. Ricardo had been weak, soft, too much like his mother in many ways. But he'd been his blood, his legacy.

As such, Castillo had tried to make a place for him in his business, though it was clear Ricardo would never rise to take his place at the top. But Ricardo had had his father's pride, and that hadn't been good enough for him. He had come to the United States to make his own name out from the shadow of his father, create his own business, prove himself worthy. Castillo had respected that, though he'd doubted Ricardo would find much success. Truth be told, it was the most he had ever respected his son.

And now Ricardo was gone. Dead. Murdered. His killer unpunished.

But not for long.

Resolve hardened in his belly, making his insides clench.

No, not for long. He was closer than ever before. The delay was temporary, that was all.

Drawing a deep breath, he surveyed the desert scene and tried to let the peacefulness of it sink into his soul.When he'd purchased this property, it hadn't been for the view. It had been for purely business purposes. The land was located in a strategic location, isolated yet near enough to the border to make a good place for the merchandise he had coming into and out of this country to pass through.

He'd never expected himself to be one of those things passing through this location, never thought he'd lay eyes on it in person. But the property had proven ideal for his current purposes, as well.

No one knew he was in this country, and no one would. As soon as this business was completed, he would slip back out of the United States as easily as he'd slipped into it.

But first he needed the Lowry woman to deliver.

He'd been able to tell from the hysteria in the woman's voice that she hadn't been lying or acting. Someone truly had shot at her to prevent her from delivering the information to him. The only positive aspect of this turn of events was that it proved there was something to hide about Ricardo's death, something someone would stop at nothing to keep hidden. It was why the Lowry woman had had her first accident, why they had tried to stop her again.

A tentative knock at the door behind him pulled him out of his thoughts. "Enter," he said without turning to see who it was.

The door softly slid open. "Do you need anything?" a voice asked moments later. Diaz.

"No," he said simply. "The girl is secure?"

"Yes."

"Good." She meant too much to the success of this mission. He knew some of the men would have enjoyed having their time with her if he'd allowed it, had seen the lust in their eyes. In many cases he wouldn't have opposed such a thing. The girl would have to be killed at the end of this, of course, as would her sister.

But he didn't want her too hurt or traumatized to speak if he needed to put her on the telephone with her sister to confirm she was alive, something that would likely be the case now that the planned exchange hadn't happened.

The rage surged anew, searing at his nerve

endings as if threatening to burst through his skin. As though he could sense it, Diaz retreated. Castillo heard the door close gently behind him.

So close. He'd been so close to getting what he needed, the name of those responsible for Ricardo's death.

Clearly someone knew it—how much they had to lose—to go to so much trouble to try and stop her.

But they would not be able to hide that information forever. No matter how hard they tried to stop her, Castillo wagered that the Lowry woman would come through in the end. He understood her perhaps better than anyone.

After all, this was about *her* family. She would do whatever she had to.

Just as he would.

PIPER SHIFTED UNEASILY in her seat as the truck barreled down the open highway toward the cowboy's ranch. She hadn't felt this uncertain when they'd been headed toward the rendezvous point. Back then, she'd had a plan. She'd known where she was going, where she had to be, what she had to do. Before that, it had all been about getting to Pam. For the past two days, she'd been running nonstop with clear objectives in mind.

Now she didn't have any of those things. She had no idea where they were going or what to do or what was going to happen next. The only thing she knew was that, once again, she wasn't calling the shots. This man was, just as the kidnapper had been. She liked the feeling even less. At least with the kidnapper, she'd known what his motives were. With this man, she didn't even have that.

She studied him out of the corner of her eye, knowing he was probably aware of her scrutiny but hoping he couldn't read her nervousness. Why would he want to help her after everything she'd done to him, knowing how much trouble she was in?

"Because somebody needs to."

It was a like a line out of a movie. People didn't say things like that in real life. People didn't *do* things like this in real life, certainly not in hers. She wanted to believe people like that did exist, that there were people who were willing to help a complete stranger, that she'd somehow come across one when she had needed him most. Experience had taught her that she couldn't. No one in her life had ever offered her as much as that, not even Pam, her supposed other half.

Could she even trust him? It might not be a

coincidence that he happened to come along when she'd been on her way to meet the kidnappers. Or even if he wasn't directly involved, he might know them. She hadn't thought Tara could trust anyone in the area, and yet here she was doing exactly that. Telling him the whole story may have been a huge mistake. She knew nothing about this man, who he associated with, what kind of life he led.

There was still time to ask him to drive her to the nearest town and let her out there, instead. She didn't know what she would do when she got there, but his reaction to the request could reveal a lot about his true intentions.

But something told her that she could trust this man. She only hoped it was gut instinct, one she could rely on, and she wasn't letting desperation cloud her mind, tricking her into placing her trust in a man she knew nothing about.

Including his name, she realized with a start. She'd been so dazed by the offer and everything that had happened in such a short amount of time she hadn't even thought to ask, simply following him back to his truck without a word. She could have shaken herself. That was definitely a mistake, potentially a fatal one. Damn. She needed to pull it together.

"What's your name?" she asked. The question came out more bluntly than she'd intended and she nearly winced. Of course, she'd pulled a gun on the man. It was a little late to worry about being rude.

If he took offense at her tone, he didn't show it. She hadn't seen a single flicker of emotion pass over the stony expression he'd worn since they'd climbed back into the truck, and she didn't now. "McClain," he said tersely. "Cade McClain."

Her automatic response upon meeting someone was usually to say it was good to meet them, and she felt the words rise to her tongue. She choked them back, knowing how ridiculous they'd sound at this point. Not to mention he probably didn't feel the same.

"How long have you lived around here?" she asked, instead.

"Four years," he said. "That's when I bought the ranch."

She glanced at him in surprise. So he really had meant it was "his" ranch, not just one where he worked. He must be successful if he'd been able to buy it four years ago when he was only in his mid-thirties.

"So you must know everybody in the area pretty well."

"Pretty much."

"Any ideas of anyone who might be involved in something like this?"

"I've been thinking about it. Haven't come up with a name yet."

Not knowing what else to say, she turned her attention back to the road in front of them. The western landscape stretched out around them, seemingly endless. She was so tired she could barely think straight. It was all she could do not to sink back into the worn leather seat and close her eyes, if only for a moment.

"This is it."

Piper jolted upright, her eyes flying open, the realization that she had closed them after all shocking her. She couldn't afford to let her guard down. Yet it appeared she just had.

They were turning onto a driveway. Directly in front of them, a wooden arch with the words Triple C Ranch carved into it curved above the road. Piper had barely taken in the words when they'd passed beneath them.

Ahead she could see a long, one-story house, a barn a short distance from it, and several smaller buildings beyond. There appeared to be a few fenced-in areas, and surrounding it was flat, open land as far as the eye could see. Piper couldn't detect any signs where the land ended. Clearly it was a massive property, she noted with a flicker of unease. She should have assumed as much. Ranches probably weren't small, not that she would know. She'd never been to one before.

They were completely isolated out here. If she wanted to leave and he refused to let her, there was likely no way for her to escape. She would be among strangers, all of whom would be his allies, not hers. Most of them probably worked for him. And even if she was right in trusting him, there were no guarantees the same applied to anyone else here. Either way, she could be trapped here with the enemy.

McClain pulled the truck to a stop in front of the house. Through the windshield she could see a man approaching the truck from the barn. Piper felt another flicker of unease. Who was he? McClain didn't appear concerned in the least, and the man was on his property, so he must be someone who belonged here. She would still feel a lot better if she knew who he was.

Before she could ask, McClain shut off the engine, unfastened his seat belt and climbed out without a word or a glance back, leaving her no choice but to follow his lead and get out.

Shading her eyes with one hand, Piper scrutinized the man approaching, trying to make a quick determination if he was friend or foe. He was a tall, muscular man, dressed in a button-down shirt, jeans and boots like McClain. Another cowboy. Piper guessed he was in his early thirties, his black hair and bronze skin indicating a Latino heritage. As he came closer, she could see he was handsome, albeit in a very different way from the man beside her.

"Everything okay?" he called. "I was expecting you back a while ago."

"Yeah, something just came up." As he said it, he turned slightly toward her, leaving no doubt what that something was. "Piper Lowry, this is my foreman, Matt Alvarez. Matt, Piper Lowry."

She felt a moment of alarm at the sound of her name leaving McClain's mouth, at having this new stranger learn who she was. Could he be trusted?

In fact, the way the man's eyes narrowed with something that looked a lot like suspicion, Piper's gut reaction was that he couldn't be. She instantly reevaluated her first impression. There was nothing handsome about the cold way he was looking at her.

"Hello," Alvarez said, not bothering to say

it was good to meet her either, since it clearly wasn't.

Piper glanced up at Cade, her body tensing in preparation to bolt if necessary, even if she didn't have any idea where she would go. "Is there a problem?"

"No," he said, glaring at the other man. "Matt is just not much of a people person. Don't mind him. Come on inside." He jerked his chin at Alvarez. "You, too. We need to talk."

Turning back to her, Cade extended his arm toward the house, motioning her to proceed. Inching forward, Piper kept her eyes on Alvarez, who stared right back with that same unrelenting suspicion. Finally she was forced to look forward and climb the front steps, Cade right behind her.

As they crossed the wide porch, Cade moved in front of her and opened the door for her. She stepped into a large entryway.

"In here." Cade motioned to a room directly to the left. "Have a seat."

It was a living room. Piper barely took note of the decor, falling into the nearest chair. It, two others and a couch were clustered around a coffee table. Each of the men took one of the other chairs.

"So what's going on?" Alvarez said before he was even in his seat.

Piper wasn't sure how much she wanted to reveal to this strangely hostile man. Cade took the decision out of her hands.

"Piper's sister has been kidnapped for ransom," he said without preamble. "Piper was ordered to drive out to Cartwright for the exchange, but had car trouble and didn't make it. I picked her up along the side of the highway, which is when somebody started shooting at us. We managed to get away, and I brought her here so we could figure out what to do."

Cade offered the sanitized version of what had happened so smoothly Piper almost could have believed it herself. From the way Alvarez's eyes narrowed again, shifting slightly from Cade to her and back again, he suspected there was more to the story, as well.

"Aren't you going to call the police?"

"No," Piper said immediately. "I can't."

Alvarez raised one eyebrow so high it nearly met his hairline. "You *can't?*"

Cade quickly explained about Pam, the fact that she was an FBI agent, and what had happened to her. "Piper doesn't know who within the FBI she can trust. There's a good chance someone there is involved and was the person shooting at us. She doesn't want to risk contacting the police and having them getting in touch with the FBI, alerting them to where she is."

"You think you can't trust the police?" Alvarez said.

"For the kidnappers to bring me here of all places, chances are they have some connection to the area. That could include anyone with the local police. I can't risk it. My sister's life is on the line. I can't afford to trust the wrong person."

"But you trust us, even though we're locals?" he asked, his voice tinged with a disbelief she understood all too well. It did seem ridiculous, that she would choose to trust a complete stranger over the police when they were just as likely to be involved with the kidnappers as anyone with the local authorities.

Her eyes immediately returned to Cade, and as she took him in once more, she realized it was true. She felt it in her bones. She did trust him. If he was involved in this, she couldn't imagine what kind of game he was playing. She'd already admitted she wasn't the sister the kidnappers were expecting, didn't have the information they wanted and likely had no way of obtaining it. He had her in his house on his vast, isolated property. No one knew where she was and likely no one could help her if she needed it. There was no reason to continue pretending he was trying to help her if he wasn't.

As for Matt Alvarez, she had to hope Cade knew him well enough to be right about him. There was no turning back now.

"I do," she said in response to Alvarez's question, directing her words at Cade so there could be no doubt who she meant. Cade gave her a small nod. The slight gesture, combined with the solemnity in his eyes, seemed to say he understood and took them as seriously as she did.

Turning back to Alvarez, she looked him straight in the eye. "If it was your sister we were talking about, is there anyone with the local police you would trust with her life?"

As soon as he grimaced, she knew she had him there, and he wasn't the least bit happy about it. "All right," he muttered. "So what *are* the two of you planning to do?"

It was a very good question, one Piper still didn't have an answer for. She glanced again at Cade. He'd suggested coming here so they could figure it out. He'd been so quiet on the drive she wondered if he'd thought of anything.

"I figure they must be keeping her somewhere nearby," Cade said slowly. "There has to be a reason they had Piper come all the way out here, and they wouldn't want to have to transport the sister far to bring her to the meeting place."

"Unless the sister's already dead and they had no intention of returning her or producing her at the meeting," Alvarez said, the words making Piper's blood run cold. "If she—" he nodded toward Piper "—came all this way and had the information on her, they would have had her cornered and there would have been no reason to hold up their end of the bargain."

"The man just told me I could talk to Tara the next time he calls, so I have to believe she's still alive. I *have* to," Piper repeated, her voice breaking slightly. She slammed her lips together as though that would somehow bring the sound back and turned her head away from both men, her eyes suddenly burning. The fact that she hadn't been able to speak to Tara yet had never been far from her thoughts, the possible implications terrifying her.

"You can believe it," Cade said quietly but firmly. "She's their leverage. They're not going to do anything to her until they have what they want."

She looked up at him. He met her gaze and nodded again, the confidence and reassurance she saw in his eyes bolstering her courage. He'd clearly read what she was thinking, and the unexpected kindness in his response surprised her, touching something deep inside her.

"All right," Alvarez said, his tone almost grudging. "So if the sister is alive where would they keep her?"

"I've been thinking about that," Cade said. "What about the Emerson spread?"

Alvarez appeared to mull this over for a moment before nodding. "I guess that makes sense."

Piper leaned forward in excitement. "Where's the Emerson spread?"

"It's the property next to mine to the east," Cade said. "Everybody else in the area has been here for years. I can't see any of them being involved in something like this. Jim Emerson had to sell last year. As far as I know, no one knows who bought the property and nobody's seen the new owners. I've heard talk there've been people out there recently though."

"I've seen movement over there," Matt confirmed. "But whoever's over there has pretty much kept to themselves. They sure haven't come over to introduce themselves, and nobody in town has met them."

"That's suspicious, isn't it?" Piper asked. "If they were living or ranching or anything out there, they would have to go into town for supplies and things, right? Unless there's a reason they're keeping a low profile."

"Most likely. Some people have been wondering if there isn't something illegal going on out there. Maybe a meth lab, or some other kind of drugs. It's also pretty easy to get to Cartwright going through the back of the property. Wouldn't even have to take any of the main roads."

"What do you want to do?" Matt asked. "Go over there and talk to them?"

"No. If it is them, I don't want to tip them off we're on to them. It'll only make them more careful than they're already being. I was thinking we should start by finding out who does own the property if we can." He raised a brow. "I thought you might give Abby a call, see if she could help you out."

The look Matt shot him said exactly what he thought of that idea. Cade didn't cave, simply looking back at him.

"Abby?" Piper asked carefully.

"She's a friend of Matt's." Cade's expression betrayed nothing, but it was pretty clear what kind of friend the woman was to Alvarez. Piper could only imagine this Abby had seen a softer side of the man than she had. She certainly hoped so.

"And she can help?"

"She works at the county clerk's office. She can tell us who the new owner is." He studied Matt. "Well?"

"Can I have a word with you first? In private?"

The look that crossed Cade's face said he wanted to say no. Piper quickly stood. It sounded like she needed this man's help, so she was willing to do whatever it took to stay on his good side. If he wanted a word with Cade alone, she could give it to him. She just prayed Cade would be able to convince him to cooperate. "I'm sorry. Is there any way I can use the bathroom?"

"Sure," Cade said, glancing back toward the entryway. "The closest one is down the hallway, third door on the right."

"Thanks."

She wasted no time making her exit, slipping out of the room.

CADE AND MATT SAT in silence staring at each other as Piper's footsteps retreated down the hallway. Cade could tell Matt was holding his tongue, just as ready to say something as Cade himself was. They waited, locked in a silent standoff.

Finally the sound of the bathroom door clicking shut down the hall reached them.

"What are you doing?" Matt said lowly before Cade could open his mouth. "Why are you getting involved in this mess?"

"Because somebody has to."

"Why does it have to be you?"

"Because I don't see anyone else, do you?"

Matt simply stared at him through narrowed eyes for a long moment before giving his head a small shake.

"What?" Cade demanded.

"I remember the last time you decided to save some woman who needed it," Matt said flatly.

The reminder sent a searing hot pain slicing through him. "This is nothing like Caitlin," Cade said. "And even it was, I sure as hell learned my lesson the last time. I'm damn well not going to make the same mistake again."

"Glad to hear it. But you're still putting yourself on the line for a woman you don't even know, and this situation's a hell of a lot more serious than that one. Somebody was shooting at you? I mean, come on. Don't you think this story is a little hard to believe?"

"Of course. But with everything I've experienced in the past hour, I know it's all true."

Matt's expression tightened with suspicion. "There's more to this than what you're telling me, isn't there?"

"I told you everything you need to know." He wasn't about to tell Matt that Piper had pulled a gun on him, that that was how they'd first met. It wasn't exactly something that would make Matt any more eager to help her, and would only further convince him that Cade was crazy for wanting to do so.

"I don't think so," Matt said. "Not if you want me to help you. Not if you're putting more people in danger than just yourself. Because that's what's happening here. You're putting everyone on this ranch in danger. If this woman has people after her, they could come here looking for her and every one of us could be at risk."

He was right, Cade conceded. It was something he hadn't really considered in the middle of trying to work out Piper's situation. But he should have. He owed it to everyone who worked for him.

"I won't expect anyone else to get involved with this. I'll give everybody a few days off with pay." It was still early in the year, and he only had a few hands working for him at the moment. In fact, it may be better that way. He might be letting Piper's paranoia get to him, but the fewer people who knew about this, the better. As long as he didn't know who was over there, he couldn't be sure who they might know and who might tell them things.

"And if this isn't resolved in a few days, what happens then?" Matt asked.

"I'll figure that out when I have to." He had enough to worry about in the present for the time being. He'd deal with the future when it came.

He did have an idea of what to do next, but wasn't ready to bring it up yet, especially since he knew what Matt's reaction would be.

"You say you don't expect anyone else to get involved in this, but you've already asked me to."

"I'm asking you to, because she needs my help and I need yours."

"You may be enough of a fool to get mixed up in this. That doesn't mean that I am."

"Are you really willing to stand by and do nothing while a young woman is being held hostage and could be killed?"

Cade saw the instant Matt relented, exactly as he'd known he would. They wouldn't have been able to work together this long if Matt was the kind of man who would stand by.

"No," Matt gritted out, his jaw tight.

"So you'll give Abby a call?" Under different circumstances, Cade might have felt bad about taking advantage of somebody's relationship like that, but with somebody's life on the line, he didn't feel an ounce of regret. Not to mention that what Matt and Abby had was no love match. It was more an arrangement between two people who had needs and no interest in settling down.

"Yeah," Matt finally relented.

The sound of footsteps drew their attention back to the hall.

Piper stood in the doorway like a skittish deer sensing danger and ready to bolt. Her eyes flicked uncertainly between him and Matt. "Everything okay?" she asked.

"Fine," Cade said. "Matt's going to give Abby a call."

The relief that poured across her face was beautiful to behold, her eyes lighting in a way he'd never seen before. The corners of her mouth turned upward in the barest hint of a smile, but coming from this woman at this moment, it was as good as if she were grinning from ear to ear. He felt a twinge of…something deep in his chest. As soon as it registered, he did his best to shake it off.

This was nothing like Caitlin. *She* was nothing like Caitlin. Caitlin would have run over to him and thrown her arms around him, pulling him to her in a stranglehold. She'd done it more than once, at least in the early days when she'd still felt gratitude toward him. She'd been prone to big, emotional gestures that had ultimately proven meaningless. This woman's reaction was much more restrained. Somehow that small smile and the look in her eyes was worth so much more.

But then, Caitlin had needed someone to save her. This woman might need help, but she was made of stronger stuff. She wasn't the kind to fall apart and need someone to solve her troubles for her. Even now, while clearly grateful, she hadn't relaxed. She stood tall, shoulders squared and head held high, as though ready to tackle whatever came at her next.

No, this woman was nothing like Caitlin. She was tougher, not to mention more loyal to those she was supposed to love.

And he wasn't going to make the damn fool mistake of getting any more involved with her than he already was.

Nope, nothing like Caitlin at all.

Chapter Six

"Why don't we go in the kitchen while Matt makes the call?" Cade suggested.

"All right," Piper agreed. As much as she wanted to learn what Matt did as soon as possible, she also didn't want to do anything to get in his way and possibly change his mind about helping.

They stepped in the hall and headed toward the back of the house where Piper had already figured the kitchen was located. "You could probably use something to eat," Cade noted.

"I'm not hungry." She couldn't even think of eating at a time like this.

"When's the last time you ate something?"

She shook her head. "I don't remember."

"That's what I figured. If you want to do your sister any good, you need to take care of yourself. You're not going to be able to do anything for her if you pass out or keel over." He shot her a dark look over his shoulder. "But I guess you're not too worried about keeling over, are you?"

Grimacing, she tried to glare back at him but he'd already turned away. She knew he didn't approve of her plan, but she knew she'd had no choice. It was the only possible chance she had to save Tara. She didn't know why he couldn't see that, but didn't really care, either. In the absence of any other options, she would make the same decisions.

He was right about one thing, though she hated to admit it. She probably did need to eat something to keep up her strength. As much as she was bothered by the idea of sitting down and eating when she could be doing something—anything—to help Tara, the last thing she needed was to get light-headed when she had to keep her wits about her to figure out what to do next.

On the way to the bathroom earlier, the mouthwatering aroma of something cooking had reached her nostrils and her stomach had immediately responded. The memory had barely returned to mind when they arrived at the kitchen, the smell hit her again, and she had the same reaction, even stronger this time.

"Supper's probably not ready," he said, the words immediately sending disappointment through her at the thought that she wouldn't be getting any of what smelled so good. "But there'll be stuff for a sandwich."

She followed him into a big, open-air space. The kitchen flowed directly into what appeared to be a full dining room, with a long wooden table big enough to fit maybe a dozen people. She wondered how many people worked for him. She could easily see the room filled with hungry ranch hands crowded at the table.

The room was empty at the moment, though somebody had to be here. Someone must be responsible for that delectable aroma that had only been making her mouth water more since they'd come in.

In an instant, she realized who it must be. Of course. A man like him, at his age and as successful as he must be with a place like this, probably would be married. He wasn't wearing a wedding ring, though that didn't necessarily mean anything. A man like him, who clearly worked outside and with his hands, may not want to wear a ring.

"Is your wife here?" she asked, curious what the woman was like. Hopefully kind enough that she wouldn't object to her husband's involvement in Piper's situation.

He actually missed a step, sending her an odd look over his shoulder.

"I don't have a wife," he said gruffly.

Good one, Piper. She felt her face burn with embarrassment. It had probably sounded like she'd been fishing for information on his marital status in the clumsiest way possible. "I'm sorry. I thought that might have been who was cooking."

"No, I have somebody to cook and clean during the day. Sharon comes in the morning to make lunch, then starts dinner cooking when she leaves in the afternoon. She has her own family to tend to in the late afternoon and evenings."

"No breakfast?"

"Usually oatmeal and eggs. I can handle that."

"You cook?" She knew as soon as the words came out of her mouth that she shouldn't have sounded as surprised as she did. Of course men cooked. She just wouldn't have imagined this man standing behind a stove. Even standing in the middle of the room, he appeared too big for this area, as though even a space this large could barely contain him. He seemed as though he belonged outdoors more, on horseback. But the image of him behind a stove, working in this kitchen, somehow made him even more appealing.

With a shrug, he reached into the refrigerator and began pulling things out. "It's just oatmeal and frying up some eggs. I can make that."

"Still, that's impressive. How many people do you have to feed?"

"Usually no more than a half dozen. Myself, Matt, a few ranch hands."

If anything she was even more impressed. "And you don't have your cook do that?"

"It's hard to find someone wanting to live all the way out here. I'm lucky to have Sharon come as far as she does."

If he had a wife, would she be expected to assume those duties? she wondered idly.

Frowning, she shook her head. Why did she even care?

"Turkey okay?"

When she saw him begin to put the sandwich together, she immediately said, "You don't have to do that."

"It's not a problem. Sandwiches, I can do. Sit."

She froze. There didn't seem to be any way to argue short of prying the sandwich fixings out of his hand, so she reluctantly settled onto the stool.

She actually liked to cook, even if she seldom bothered anymore with no one but herself to cook for. She watched him work, those long fingers moving nimbly. He had big hands, undeniably strong and perfectly formed.

He'd just placed the plate in front of her when Matt entered the kitchen.

"The ranch is owned by a corporation of some sort," he announced. "Golden Sun. Abby says that's the name on the paperwork filed with the county. There's no actual person listed."

"What about a phone number?"

"No."

Cade looked at Piper. "Does that mean anything to you? Golden Sun?"

"No, nothing." She grimaced. The information might prove to be useful in the future, but at the moment it appeared to be a dead end.

"So what do you want to do now?" Matt asked.

Cade was silent for a moment, as though mulling it over. Finally he said, "I'll go there and check it out."

Matt's mouth fell open. Piper's own nearly did the same. "I thought you didn't want to tip them off," Matt said.

"I don't. I'm thinking I'll go in tonight after

midnight, and see if I can find any sign of Piper's sister."

"Come on," Matt scoffed. "You have to know how crazy that is. If the kidnappers are there, they're probably armed and on alert, not to mention some very bad guys who won't hesitate to shoot first and ask questions later. They'll probably get away with it too since you'll be trespassing on their land."

"I know the property pretty well. We both do. We helped Emerson out from time to time, have been in the house. I bet I know it a hell of a lot better than whoever's over there now. I should be able to get in and out without them noticing."

Hope blossomed anew at his words. Piper certainly understood Matt's objections. The idea sounded risky as hell. But listening to the confidence in Cade's voice, seeing the certainty on his face as he justified his plan, she found it hard not to buy into it, especially when she desperately wanted to. This was the best chance she'd had to save Tara. As dangerous and reckless as it likely was, it was a better bet than the plan she'd been forced to come up with for the rendezvous, and in this case she wouldn't be on her own. She would have this man on her side, and it seemed like he was exactly the person anyone would want there.

She found herself studying him again with a combination of amazement and disbelief. He wasn't simply offering to help her. He was outright putting his own safety on the line for someone he didn't even know.

Who *was* this man?

Matt's voice cut through her thoughts. "You've already made up your mind about this, haven't you?" he said flatly, his expression hard as stone.

Cade looked back at him, unrepentant. "Yes."

"Then I guess there's nothing I can say." Shaking his head, Matt brushed by them and pushed through the back door.

A heavy silence fell after his departure. "Are you sure you want to do this?" Piper asked quietly in the wake of the man's absence.

"Yes," Cade said simply, without the slightest hint of doubt or hesitation.

"All right. Then I'm coming with you."

Cade immediately began to shake his head. "No way."

"I wasn't asking. I'm going."

"And I'm not joking around. You're not. It's too dangerous."

"But not for you?"

"Like I said, I know the property. You don't.

It'll be much easier for one person to get in and out undetected than two."

"It'll also be safer if someone has your back. You can't keep an eye out in every direction at all times. Not to mention that if you do find Tara, she may not trust you or that you're there to save her. Who knows what mental state she's in? But if I'm there, she'll automatically come with us without question."

"What if the kidnapper calls? You need to be available to answer the phone, and you can't have it on and with you when we're over there."

"He's not going to call in the middle of the night."

"You should stay where it's safe. Your sister needs you too much for you to put yourself in danger."

"My sister needs someone on this mission who is willing to do anything to save her. I believe you have the best intentions, but if it comes to a choice between your life and hers, you're going to choose your own, which you should. You have no reason to be that invested in rescuing her. I'm thankful enough that you're willing to do this much. But you've probably figured out by now that I will do whatever it takes to save her. That's how much she means to me."

He stared at her, his brow furrowing. "Why do you think your sister's life is worth so much more than yours?"

"I don't."

"You seem awfully willing to throw it away to save her."

She choked back a sigh of frustration. "You don't understand."

"You're right," he said bluntly. "I don't."

"Don't you have any family, people that you would do anything for?"

"No," he said dully. "I don't."

The answer wasn't what she was expecting. Of course not everyone had family, but with a house this big she'd assumed he must, that he would understand what those kind of family ties were like. But from the shuttered look in his eyes and his flat response, it seemed clear that he didn't.

"I'm sorry," she said softly. "Maybe if I tell you about my family you'll understand."

His expression said he doubted it, but he didn't object.

Piper swallowed the lump that rose in her throat at the onslaught of memories and tried to figure out where to begin. "My family was pretty normal until the year Pam and I were twelve. It was my dad, my mom and the two of us for most of those years. Pam and I were eleven when Tara was born. She was an unplanned surprise, but my parents were happy to have another child and Pam and I were thrilled to have a little sister. If anything our family seemed better than ever.

"Then my father died. It was a huge shock. He walked into a convenience store robbery and was shot and killed. One moment he was there, and then he wasn't. That's when everything changed. My mother was the kind of person who couldn't handle being alone. The three of us weren't enough for her. She needed a man in her life, so she immediately set about trying to find a new one. I think my father hadn't even been gone a month when the parade of men in our home began. She almost never introduced us. I'd like to think it was about protecting us, but I'm sure it had more to do with the fact that a lot of men don't want to get saddled with someone else's children, so she was in no rush to have them learn about us. Most of them were just vague faces Pam and I glimpsed when we peeked out our window as they left. I remember seeing the look on my mother's face one time when one of them left, the open, desperate hope that he might be the one. He wasn't, of course. And a few nights later there was someone else."

Whenever Piper thought of her mother anymore, that was what she saw—that desperate, pathetic longing on her face, the sheer need for this man to love her. She'd promised herself a long time ago she was never going to be that needy, never be so desperate to have a man. And she hadn't, perhaps a little too well, she acknowledged with a pang. She'd never wanted to need a man, but she'd probably done such a good job guarding her heart she'd never been open to letting one into her life, either. None of her relationships had lasted very long, something that had never really bothered her all that much. She'd told herself she was too busy anyway, had too much on her plate, but deep down, she knew there was more to it than that.

Not wanting to linger on that subject, Piper made herself continue. "It was up to Pam and me to keep Tara quiet when my mother had company. We took care of her most of the time, and our mother too whenever her latest romance came to an end."

"Some mother," he muttered, shaking his head.

"She wasn't a bad person, not really. She was just really sad and needy. If my father hadn't died and she still had him, she would have been fine, and everything would have been okay."

"Doesn't excuse treating her kids like that," he said with a trace of anger.

"No, it doesn't," she agreed. "But Pam and I had each other, and Tara, and we took care of each other—and a lot of the time, our mother.

"Then in high school, Pam started to pull away. She spent more and more time away from home, at friends' houses or staying late at school. I didn't really realize it was happening at first. That seems so strange to admit. She's my twin sister, the person I'd always been closest to in the whole world. But I was so busy with my own schoolwork and picking up the slack with Tara. And one day I realized I didn't really know her anymore. She had this whole other life going on, away from the family, apart from me. She wanted to get away from our miserable family life, had plans for college and attending an out-of-state school. All that work paid off. She got a scholarship to college and was able to leave."

"What about you?"

"I didn't have time to work that hard. I ended up staying home. It was better that way. Someone needed to take care of Tara and our mother. I studied accounting and was able to get a good job, which paid well. That was definitely a good thing when our mother died and it was just Tara and me."

"When was that?"

"Pam and I were twenty-two and Tara was eleven."

"What about Pam?"

"She sent money every month, which meant a lot because she was just getting started herself and didn't have much, and she'd call regularly. But she was busy building her career and wasn't really around."

"So you basically raised Tara on your own."

"Pretty much."

"She's not just your sister. She's practically your daughter."

Piper didn't know why it was so hard to admit. "In a lot of ways, yes." She was the one who'd read Tara bedtime stories, who'd packed her lunches and made her dinners, who'd watched her grow from the baby she and Pam had cared for to the young woman she almost couldn't believe was the same person. "So you can see why she means so much to me."

His expression said he did, and wasn't happy about it.

"Please," she said simply. "Let me come. I can be an asset, not a burden. Besides, I can take care of myself. I think I've proven I'm fully capable of using a gun."

"Yeah, I know," he said wryly. "Were you ever in law enforcement like your sister?"

"No. Like I said, I'm an accountant."

He frowned. "An accountant," he repeated flatly. "How did you learn how to use a gun?"

"I learned so I'd know how to protect myself. By the time I was eighteen I was taking care of myself, a little girl and a woman who couldn't take care of herself half the time. I needed to be able to keep us safe. I've taken regular target practice so I don't get rusty."

"Can you even ride?"

His words stopped her cold. She hadn't considered that. "Do I need to? You're not going to ride over there on horseback, are you? They'd hear you coming."

"I can't go on foot. If I do find your sister, I'm going to need to get out of there as quickly as possible, and a truck will be too much trouble to maneuver over that terrain. If anything, being on horseback will give me an advantage if they come after me in a vehicle. I can ride in as close as I can without them hearing me, then go in the rest of the way on foot from there."

"And what if Tara's too weak or injured to run?" Piper couldn't help but wince at the thought. "How are you going to get back to your horse quickly then?"

He thought for only a second. "I'll carry her if I have to," he said, every word sounding like a promise.

The certainty in his voice strengthened her confidence in his dedication to the mission, but didn't shake her conviction that she needed to be there. "Then you'll definitely need someone watching your back. How are you going to handle a gun and keep an eye out if you're carrying her in your arms?"

The heavy frown that fell over his face told her he didn't have an easy answer for that one. "You're right. It is a two person job. I'll ask Matt to come along." He speared her with a pointed look. "That doesn't mean you are."

"Do you really think he'll agree?" she said skeptically.

"I'll convince him."

Remembering the look on the man's face and his parting words, Piper had her doubts about that. And even if Matt did agree to go, she suspected he'd try to talk Cade into abandoning the mission at the first sign of trouble. No, she had to be there, believing it more than ever.

She scrambled for a fresh argument, inspiration quickly striking. "Who's going to watch the horses?" she asked. "If you and Matt approach the house, are you just going to leave the horses alone in the middle of nowhere?"

He shot her a look of disbelief. "You offering to come along to watch them?"

"No, Matt can watch them while I go with you to the house."

"You can't ride."

"Neither can Tara. If you're talking two horses, then there's room for each of us to ride with one of you."

He fell silent, his frown deepening. She could see him trying to come up with another argument. She spoke quickly before he could.

"Please. You know this really isn't Matt's fight, any more than it's yours. It's mine. I feel bad enough that you're involved in this. It's not fair to ask him to risk his life more than is absolutely necessary, especially when I'm willing to do this. Especially when you know how much Tara means to me and how much I'm willing to do to save her. *Please.*"

Not knowing what else to say, she simply sat there, looking at him. He remained silent for a long moment, surveying her steadily.

"Fine," he finally said, sounding anything but pleased. "We'll go together."

Relief poured through her. She opened her

mouth to thank him, only to think better of it and swallow the words. The unhappy look on his face told her that he wouldn't want to hear it.

He continued, "You should get some rest. It looks like it's going to be a long night for both of us."

Piper started to object. She didn't want to rest. She wanted to talk about what they would do. Besides, she had too much excited energy to even think of sleeping right now.

Then she felt the exhaustion that the adrenaline had been keeping at bay, and she realized he was right. If they were going to do this, she needed to be as alert as possible. As hard as it was to believe that she would be able to sleep with Tara still out there, still being held and enduring God-only-knew-what, the best thing she could do for her sister at this moment was to rest.

"Good idea," she said.

"Come on," he said, jerking his head toward the hallway. "There are plenty of open rooms. You can use any of them." She'd just started to rise when he reached over and picked up the plate in front of her. The sandwich, she suddenly remembered. She hadn't taken a single bite. He handed her the plate. "Take this. You still need it, too."

Normally being told what to do would have raised her hackles, but there was nothing bossy in the way he said it, just a kind of gruff concern that almost seemed to embarrass him. He didn't even look at her as he said it or offered her the plate, his eyes slightly lowered. Something about that brought a slight smile to her lips.

As soon as she'd taken the plate, he headed toward the hallway, leaving her to follow. They moved back down the hall along the rear of the house. He opened the second door on the left, then stepped out of the doorway to let her pass.

As expected, it was a bedroom, plainly but comfortably furnished. She immediately zeroed in on the bed. It called to her, her body ready to lurch over to it and collapse completely. She was both tense enough that it felt like she'd never fall asleep and so exhausted it seemed like she could sleep for days.

"Bathroom's right there if you need it," he said, gesturing toward one of the doors.

"Thanks."

She started to step into the room, then hesitated and turned back to at him. "You won't try to leave without me, will you?"

She was reassured by his obvious surprise. The idea clearly hadn't even occurred to him.

"No," he said. "I won't."

She believed him. She may not understand why he'd agreed to help her, but she believed he really wanted to, and she believed him now. It felt strange to trust anyone as much as she did this man, especially someone she'd known for such a short amount of time. It was a completely new feeling, but she had to admit, a good one.

"Thank you," she said again.

She wasn't surprised when he ducked his head and nodded tightly, as though brushing off her gratitude. "Sure," he said, immediately turning to head back down the hall.

Piper watched him go, that large frame seeming to fill up the hallway. He moved with an easy, self-assured stride, the sight filling her with confidence, in this plan, in him. Everything about him spoke of a man used to being in charge, to getting things done.

She could only pray he was the right man to help her get this done.

Tara's life depended on it.

Chapter Seven

As soon as he left Piper, Cade headed outside to the barn. He still couldn't really believe what he'd just agreed to. Letting her come along was probably just the latest in the series of bad ideas he'd had in the past few hours. But the more he learned about this woman, the more he understood her devotion to her sister, the harder it was to refuse.

He wished he hadn't told her that he wouldn't leave without her. Actually he really wished he'd thought of the idea first. It would have been easier to just go alone and deal with her anger when he returned, hopefully with her sister. Any negative emotion she felt would certainly be washed away if he brought her sister back, and then the whole thing would be over.

But he wouldn't have felt right lying to her. She needed someone to trust, and it was clear she'd decided to put her faith in him. He hadn't wanted to break that confidence so soon. Not to mention he didn't like the idea of leaving her here, going out of her mind wondering what was happening. There was no telling how she might react. She was so determined, he wouldn't be surprised if she tried to follow.

No, he wouldn't leave without her, which meant they really were going to undertake this incredibly risky plan together.

But she was right about one thing. If they did this, they would need help.

He found Matt in the barn exactly as he'd expected. Matt was saddling one of the horses, his back to Cade, who stood there and watched for a moment, considering the best way to approach this.

Matt was the closest thing he had to a friend in this world. They'd worked together on the last ranch Cade had worked before he'd finally saved enough money to buy his own place. Matt was the first person he'd hired after he bought the ranch, and he'd been here all this time. There was no one Cade trusted more, and no one else he'd want having his back, especially when he was about to do something as foolish as this.

Matt grunted. "You going to say something or just stand there forever?"

"I need you on this," Cade said simply.

"Too bad I'm not as crazy as you are."

"I know what I'm asking, but we can't do this ourselves."

"We?" Matt repeated with that same incredulous tone it seemed he'd been using for the past hour. He stopped what he was doing, glancing at Cade over his shoulder. "You're taking her with you?"

"She can take care of herself, and she made some good points about why she needs to be there. Not to mention, I don't want to leave her here alone in case someone comes looking for her. Whoever was shooting at us could have gotten my license plate number and would be able to figure out where I live."

"I would have thought you'd ask me to stay here with her."

"If we do find the sister, I'm going to need help getting her out of there. This is more than a one-man operation."

Matt grimaced before shaking his head. "You really are crazy," he muttered, turning his attention back to the horse. "Which is why you need somebody with you on this—somebody who knows what he's doing."

It was as good as saying yes, and Cade knew he didn't have to ask any further. He didn't bother acknowledging what they both knew, aware that Matt wouldn't want him to. They'd said enough.

"We've got plenty of daylight left," Cade said. "Anything I need to know about that happened while I was gone or anything that needs to be taken care of now?"

They went over ranch business for a while. There didn't seem to be any pressing matters that needed to be dealt with at the moment. Matt had everything well in hand, as Cade had known he would. Matt finally took off on a ride that Cade knew had just as much to do with giving himself time to clear his head and think as it did about checking things out around the ranch.

Cade wouldn't have minded taking a ride himself. God knew he could use the time and space to breathe and ponder. It felt like he hadn't been able to truly do either for the past few hours, ever since the moment he'd found himself staring down the barrel of Piper's gun.

At the reminder, he realized he still had her pistol stuck in the back of his waistband. Strange how he'd gotten so used to the feeling of it there. He pulled it out, examining it and testing the weight of it in his hand. He owned a few himself, though he was more used to rifles than handguns. Rifles would probably serve

him and Matt better when they visited the ad-
joining ranch.

Two men with rifles and a woman with a
handgun, against an unknown number of
people who were, in all likelihood, very well-
armed.

Matt was right. It was crazy. He knew it. He
also understood it was the best plan available
to them.

Before heading into the house, Cade decided
to pull his truck around the back. If anyone
stopped by—especially anyone looking for
Piper—he didn't want to have to try and explain the bullet holes in the side panel or the
blown-out back window.

Once inside, Cade headed into his office. He
should probably get some rest, too, needed it
as much as Piper did. It was going to be a long
night and he would have to be as alert as possible.

One look at all the paperwork piled up and
waiting for him confirmed that wasn't an
option.

Sighing, he moved to the desk. He'd always
dreamed of owning his own spread, had worked
his tail off and saved every last cent to make
it happen when he was still young enough to
enjoy it. He loved it, loved the work, loved the

land. The paperwork, on the other hand, he could do without.

Taking a seat, he carefully set Piper's gun on the desk beside him and got to work.

It felt like he'd barely started when someone knocked on the door frame.

He jerked up his head to find Matt standing in the doorway. "What is it?"

"Trouble," Matt said bluntly. "You should come out."

Cade wasted no time getting up, sparing a glance at the clock. Damn. Nearly three hours had passed. "What's going on?"

"We've got company."

Cade didn't bother asking what kind of company. It was pretty clear it wasn't the good kind. He immediately reached for the gun, then moved to the door.

Matt was waiting for him in the entryway. He nodded toward the open front door.

"Who is it?" Cade asked.

"Says he's with the FBI."

Frowning, Cade shoved the gun into the back of his waistband. They may have reasons to distrust anyone from the FBI at the moment, but going out to meet a federal agent with a gun in hand probably wasn't the best idea. If whoever was out there really was a federal agent. Either way, he wasn't going completely unarmed.

Moments later they both stepped onto the porch. Cade immediately saw the man standing at the bottom of the steps. Dressed in a dark suit and sunglasses, he was in his late thirties, with thinning blond hair and soft, bland features. Cade had never seen him before.

Cade stopped at the edge of the porch and looked at the man. "Can I help you?"

The man removed his sunglasses, then reached into his jacket and pulled out an ID, holding it out to Cade. "Special Agent Jay Larson. I'm with the FBI. This is your ranch?"

"That's right."

"And you are?" the man said when Cade didn't continue.

"McClain. Cade McClain."

"Mr. McClain, I'm looking for a woman named Piper Lowry. Her sister is a federal agent suspected of stealing classified information, and we believe Piper Lowry may be involved and on her way to deliver the information to the highest bidder. I've been following her trail and managed to track her to the area. Her rental car was found abandoned along the side of the highway several miles back, but there was no sign of her. Looks like she may have had engine trouble.

Most likely she was either picked up by someone she came here to meet, or she managed to catch a ride with someone. I'm just checking if anyone in the area has seen her."

The man sounded convincing enough that Cade would have had no trouble believing him if he hadn't met Piper himself. He wondered if it was because Larson really did believe what he was saying, or if he was just a good liar.

"No, I haven't," Cade said.

The man cocked his head slightly, his smile unwavering. "I haven't told you what she looks like."

"Doesn't matter," Cade returned without missing a beat. "I haven't seen any women I don't know. Any women at all today for that matter."

"Mind if I leave you my card, Mr. McClain? If you do see her, I'd appreciate you letting me know."

Unable to think of any reason to refuse, Cade said, "Sure," and accepted the card Larson held out to him.

Larson looked him straight in the eye, his expression sobering. "She's a dangerous woman, Mr. McClain. She and her sister have gotten involved with some unsavory characters. She's also an accomplished liar and you can't trust a word she says. If you do see her, please contact me. Everyone will be better off when she's in custody."

"Sounds like it," Cade said mildly.

With a curt nod, the man turned on his heel and headed for a dark blue sedan parked a few yards away. A car with no noticeable damage, Cade noted, remembering Piper's suspicions that whoever had been shooting at them was with the FBI. Of course, the lack of damage didn't necessarily mean anything. The man would have had time to get a replacement vehicle by now.

Cade stayed where he was as the man climbed back into the sedan. As soon as the car door shut, Cade turned toward Matt. The engine didn't immediately start, and Cade figured Larson was watching him. Better to appear that the man's visit hadn't meant anything to him, exactly how someone would react if he hadn't met Piper and didn't know what was really going on here. Still, he listened carefully, not about to let down his guard in the least.

Finally the sound of the engine starting met his ears. He remained where he was, listening as the car reversed and turned around before heading down the driveway. Eventually it reached the main road and fell out of earshot.

"Think that guy's really a Fed?" Matt asked under his breath.

"I don't know. Could be."

Matt grunted his agreement. "So what do you want to do now?"

Cade looked up into the distance, where the sun was sliding under the horizon, the sky blazing red and orange. It was getting late. They didn't have time to worry about Larson or whoever he was at the moment.

Larson's visit had served one purpose at least—reminding Cade of Piper's rental car. It was still sitting along the side of the highway. They needed to do something about that. If anyone local reported it to the authorities, he could have more visitors dropping by looking for the driver. More important, if they did get her sister back, the two of them were going to need a way to leave here. If she called and reported the damage, the rental company would no doubt send some people out to drop off a new one and pick up her old one. He or Matt could go out and meet whoever it was to make the exchange for Piper, then they could hide the car in the barn until it was time for her to leave. Something else they would need to take care of.

"It's going to be dark soon," Cade said. "We need to start planning for tonight."

CADE DIDN'T HAVE TO WORRY about waking Piper. He had just reemerged from his office at the other end of the hall when she came out of her room.

She still looked exhausted. He was tempted to tell her to try to get a few more hours' rest, but figured there was no point when he knew she wasn't going to agree to it.

"What's going on?"

He quickly explained about their visitor. "Have you heard of him?"

Her brow furrowed. "No, the name isn't familiar. I wonder if he was the shooter."

"Could have been. The car he was driving didn't have any damage, but he could have gotten a replacement by now."

"So what now?"

He held up the large rolled-up paper in his right hand that he'd just retrieved from the office. "We need to plan our approach for tonight."

"Then it looks like I got up just in time."

"I guess so. Matt's waiting in the kitchen."

Some of the weariness evaporated from her face, replaced by surprise. "So he's coming?"

"He's agreed to help," Cade confirmed.

They moved into the kitchen, where Matt stood at the counter pouring two cups of coffee. He looked up as they entered, his eyes moving to Piper. His expression giving away nothing, he acknowledged her with a short nod. All he said was "Coffee?"

Piper was clearly caught off guard by the offer and Matt's unexpected courtesy, but managed a weak smile.

"That would be great," she murmured. "Thanks."

He nodded again and retrieved a third mug. Cade moved to the dining room table and unfurled the paper in his hand on the wide surface. The surveyor's map showed both his land and the property next to it, with the buildings on each clearly outlined. Cade knew all of it like the back of his hand, but figured it would help to have the visual in front of him while trying to work this out. Piper should see it, too. She needed to have some idea where they were going.

The others quickly joined him, Piper setting a mug within his reach.

"Thanks," he said. "Okay, I was thinking we'd go in here." He pointed to a spot on the border between his land and his neighbor's. "It won't take too long to reach from our side, but is far enough from the house on their side that they shouldn't see us coming. I haven't noticed any extra security measures between our properties, have you?"

Matt shook his head. "No."

"I doubt they've done anything. There's so much land along the perimeter that it would have taken them long enough to set up something that we would have noticed them working out there. We'll still have to be careful and check when we arrive, but I doubt we'll have any problems." If they had had the time, he would have scoped things out. But it was getting late, and it would be dark soon. And on the off chance anyone was checking the boundaries, he didn't want them to spot him. The last thing he needed was to give his new neighbors more reason to be on guard when the three of them infiltrated the ranch.

"How are you thinking of going in? On foot? It's a long walk to the house."

"No, on horseback. Piper can ride with me."

"They'll hear us coming," Matt said.

"Not if we don't ride in the whole way," Cade said. "We'll stop far enough from the buildings out of earshot and proceed afterward on foot."

"What about the horses?" Matt asked.

"You'll stay with them. Piper and I will go in and try to find her sister."

"You don't want some kind of backup with you?"

"Piper has a gun," Cade said, causing Matt to glance at her. "If you and I have rifles, we should be covered as much as we can be."

"Do you know where we should look?" Piper asked.

"I have an idea," Cade replied. "Like I said, I know the ranch well. If they are holding her, they'll want her to be close at hand. They'll probably be staying in the house. No reason for them not to. Which means they'll either have her in there with them, or possibly the barn."

"The barn should be easy enough to get into," Matt said. "The house will be trickier."

"It doesn't have a security system," Cade said.

"They could have upgraded," Matt pointed out. "Setting up extra fencing or alarms along the perimeter is one thing, but adding security to the house wouldn't be that hard."

"They could have," Cade agreed. "We'll have to be careful. I don't see them going to all that trouble though. They would have had no reason to believe anyone had any idea what they're up to out there, and I'm assuming they're armed. Still, we'll be careful."

"Obviously," Matt said in a tone dry as dust. "What happens if you find the sister?"

"If we find her, we'll have to get her out."

"She may be in no position to run if they've had her tied up for several days," Matt said.

"Between the two of us, Piper and I should be able to get her to you and the horses. Tara can ride back with you, and we'll get the hell out of there."

The room fell into silence. Cade could see Matt going over the plan in his head.

"It's crazy," Matt finally declared. "But it could work."

Cade glanced at Piper, reading the worry and determination in her eyes and knowing exactly what she was thinking.

Yes, the plan *could* work.

But more important, it had to.

Chapter Eight

They left the house shortly after 1:00 a.m.

Piper watched Cade and Matt saddle two horses in the barn. She'd never been on a horse before and couldn't help but feel a little trepidation at doing so for the first time. She wasn't sure she'd ever even seen a horse in real life. They were massive, towering over the men. Still, compared to everything else she needed to worry about in the next several hours, riding a horse was nothing, and for Tara she wouldn't hesitate to do it.

Once Cade and Matt were done and had loaded their packs, they led the horses out of the barn, stopping just in front of the building. Cade motioned her forward, extending his hand. "Ladies first."

Piper inched forward. "What do I do?" she murmured, feeling foolish for having to ask.

"Hold on here," he said, placing a hand on

the front of the saddle. "Put your right foot in the stirrup, and I'll help you up."

She did as instructed. It was only when her foot was in the stirrup and she suddenly felt his hands on her hips that she realized what he meant by helping her up. Then he was lifting her, his hands strong and firm on her body. When she was standing in the stirrup she instinctively threw her other leg over the saddle until she could lower herself into it.

There. That wasn't so hard.

Then it was his turn. She removed her foot from the stirrup to allow him access to it. Moments later he swung himself into the saddle behind her.

His hips landed against her backside and she instinctively tried to move forward a little to give him more room. There certainly wasn't much available. Then his arms went around her as he picked up the reins, and there was suddenly even less room.

Her nervousness about being on the animal was forgotten, replaced by a new source that had her heart pounding faster and the adrenaline pumping through her system. Because she was aware of just how close they were sitting, his hard chest pressed against her back, his thighs cradling her hips. She'd known they would be riding together, but somehow she'd never thought about how they would be positioned. Now that she was experiencing it, she couldn't think of anything else. She barely felt the massive, living, breathing animal under her. She only felt the very human animal behind her.

"You okay?" he asked quietly, again surprising her with his nearness as his warm breath brushed against her ear.

She wondered at first if he could tell how she was responding to him, to his touch, then realized he was probably just being considerate and ensuring she was comfortable before they left.

"Yes," she whispered back, her voice thankfully steady.

"Good," he said. "Then let's go."

He spurred the horse into motion. Piper glanced over to see Matt on his own horse, alongside them.

They began at an easy walk, moving behind the house and barn. Once there, Cade and Matt seemed to share some silent cue. Cade prompted the horse again, and it took off at a trot, then, what seemed like mere moments later, at an all-out run.

Piper held on to the front of the saddle in a death grip, her heart racing as fast as the horse beneath her. She was bombarded by impressions, too different and too many for her to absorb. The sound of hoofbeats was deafening, filling the night to surround her. It seemed too loud, as though there was no way the people on the neighboring ranch wouldn't be able to hear them coming, though she knew Cade and Matt wouldn't be going this fast if there was any chance that was the case. The landscape seemed to fly by too fast for her to see any of it, just flat earth and pale moonlight.

Then she felt Cade's arms locked around her, securing her in the saddle. She gradually let herself sink into the sensation of those arms, of his strong chest behind her, letting them steady her. With him holding her, the ride suddenly seemed less overwhelming. She let herself breathe in the feeling. The roar of the horses' hooves hitting the ground faded, and the world before her came into focus.

The moon shone down on the landscape, casting everything in a silvery glow. The land was flat and dotted with small plants and shrubs tough enough to survive in the arid climate, but undeniably beautiful in the moonlight. It was so different from where she had come from, like she'd truly entered another world. There was something so unreal about this moment, so different from her everyday life, racing across the desert, held tightly against a man she had just met but somehow trusted.

Piper was sure they knew where they were going, but she could hardly tell any difference in the landscape. She just sat back and tried to take it in.

Her first indication they were nearing the end of Cade's land was when the horses suddenly began to slow. They didn't stop entirely, moving back into a trot as they continued forward.

It wasn't long before Piper spotted the fence up ahead. They stopped a few feet from it. Matt quickly swung himself off his horse and moved to the fence, producing a small flashlight from his pocket. Switching it on, he waved it over the fence and the surrounding ground, no doubt looking for any signs of a security system. Evidently not finding any, he turned off the flashlight and returned to his horse, pulling a heavy pair of gloves from the pockets of his jacket and tugging them on. Reaching into the pack tied to his horse, he retrieved a pair of metal cutters, then moved again to the fence. Working as quickly as possible, he cut through the barbed wire, then peeled it back, creating a big enough gap for the horses to get through easily.

Before Matt was reseated on his horse, Cade urged his through the opening and onto the other side. Piper braced herself for something to happen, for an alarm that Matt had missed to sound now that they were breaching enemy territory.

Nothing happened. They passed through without incident, then waited on the other side for Matt to remount his horse and follow them.

Once he had, she expected them to begin moving again. They didn't, continuing to wait for a short time. Piper could sense Cade listening carefully. She did the same.

She heard nothing, only her heart thudding frantically and the whistle of the night wind surrounding them.

Finally, having evidently determined it was safe to proceed, Cade prompted the horse to start moving again.

She still couldn't let herself relax. If anything, her tension only grew the farther they traveled into possible danger. She couldn't see any sign of the buildings they were heading toward up ahead, only the same flat, open terrain they'd passed through on Cade's side.

Cade spurred the horse to move faster without breaking into an outright run. The sound of hooves hitting the packed earth still sounded impossibly loud in the eerie stillness of the night.

The landscape passed in a blur, Piper's heart beating faster than ever, until they slowed again. She still didn't see any buildings in front of them.

She gradually came to realize it wasn't just her own heart she could feel pounding. It was Cade's, moving slightly off tempo with hers. With their bodies pressed together and only a few layers of clothes between them, she was aware of his heart thudding against her back, his pulse racing in the arms that held her. Somehow that made the closeness even more intimate. There was something soothing about it, their hearts beating together, gradually calming her nerves.

They finally came to a stop, seemingly in the middle of nowhere. There was still nothing in sight in front of them, just open land illuminated by moonlight.

Cade set down the reins in front of her. She felt him climbing out of the saddle, followed by the sound of his boots hitting the dirt moments later. She looked down to find him setting his rifle on the ground, then he reached for her, his hands settling again on her hips with disconcerting familiarity. He met her eyes and nodded once, asking if she was ready. She jammed her foot in the stirrup and nodded in return. It felt as though she didn't have to do anything as he helped her down from the horse, lifting her with the utmost ease and then lowering her to the ground.

Once she was on her feet, Cade turned and picked up his rifle. Seeing it in his hands, Piper pulled her gun from the inside of her jacket. It felt good in her hand, and though she'd checked it before they'd left the house, she did an automatic recheck to make sure it was ready, more than prepared to use it if necessary.

Once she'd determined it was good to go, she glanced up to find him watching her. He nodded once, again asking if she was ready. She returned the nod, a confirmation. With one last nod to Matt, Cade started walking. Piper immediately fell into line behind him.

They moved quietly, their feet barely making any sounds on the ground. Cade kept his body slightly hunched, as though trying to make himself smaller and less noticeable. She wasn't sure that was possible, she thought with a sudden pang of fear, but hoped he knew better than she did.

They'd walked at least ten minutes before Piper spotted the vague shape of buildings up ahead. As they moved closer, Piper was able to discern the house and barn. Her pulse kicked up a notch. This was it. Tara was most likely in one of those buildings. She had to be. So close…

She finally realized that one of the lights she was seeing wasn't a star on the horizon, it was coming from the yard. There was a single light on a post in the yard between the house and barn, casting light in a wide circle between the two buildings. There appeared to be several vehicles parked in front of the house, though Piper couldn't make them out clearly.

Cade stopped and motioned toward her, gesturing to the rear of the barn.

She nodded her understanding. Instead of approaching directly, he wanted to work their way to the back of the barn, then come around the side. It made sense. They would be able to remain in semidarkness longer, and especially avoid that spotlight in the yard. They'd have to deal with it eventually, but the longer they put it off, the better. Now that they were this close to the house, she felt painfully exposed just in the moonlight.

They made their way quickly, Piper doing her best to remain within a few feet of him, all the while keeping an eye out for any activity in the area around the residence. She saw none. It was a one-story house a little smaller than Cade's. No lights were on from this side. With any luck that would mean everyone was asleep. It had to be after two by now. That would certainly make things a lot easier.

There was a fence surrounding a pasture at the rear of the barn. They ducked beneath it and moved straight to the building. The large door at the back was slightly ajar. Moving his rifle to one hand, Cade produced a flashlight, using it to peer through the opening, then quickly slipped inside. Piper waited nervously, scanning the area, clutching her Glock in front of her. She didn't expect anyone else to be approaching the barn from this side at this time of night, but she couldn't afford to take any chances.

A flash of motion in the corner of her eye drew her attention again to the door. A hand had emerged—Cade's—and was waving her forward. Pushing down a sigh of relief, she backed through the door, keeping her eyes peeled in front of her.

Once inside, they began to walk the length of the barn. Cade's posture relaxed the tiniest bit, at least in comparison to before. She peered in the stalls and every available door. It didn't take her long to determine what he must have, why he'd relaxed a little. There was nothing here. The stalls were empty. There were no horses, no other animals. The building remained unnaturally still, the silence cavernous around them.

Whatever the people here were doing, it didn't seem to involve animals, which did seem suspicious. More evidence that the ranch was being used for something shady?

The barn, on the other hand, wasn't being used at all, she realized.

They reached the end of the barn. She and Cade exchanged a nod, having reached the same conclusion.

Tara wasn't here.

Time to move to the house.

She swallowed at the thought. This was where things really got tricky. She didn't know how many men would be in the house. How many would they consider necessary to guard one young woman? Four? Six? A full dozen?

It appeared they would find out.

Cade turned and gestured for them to go back the way they'd come. It was the sensible course of action. If they went out the front, they'd be caught in the big light and plainly visible from the house. Better to go out the back of the barn and continue circling around to the other side of the house, which would hopefully be as dark.

They did just that. The part of the barn they hadn't been on was the darkest yet, casting a long shadow the moonlight didn't pierce. It was almost like moving in complete darkness. Piper had to stick close to Cade, sensing him more than she saw him.

When they made it to the front and cleared the barn's massive shadow, they paused at the edge of the building before moving forward to the house. It was as she'd guessed. The rear of the house was just as dark, with no light on outside and none inside shining outward. The house itself seemed about a mile away.

Without looking back at her, Cade pointed to the house, then held up three fingers, lowering them one by one. A countdown.

It could only mean one thing.

He was telling her to get ready to run.

She braced herself, her muscles tensing in readiness.

Three. Two.

One.

The finger had barely lowered when he took off, the rifle falling into place, held in front of him and ready to be aimed and fired. Piper wasted no time following suit, breaking into an all-out run, swiveling from side to side to look around herself in case anyone should appear, the Glock primed in front of her.

Then they were at the house. Both breathing

heavily but silently, they pressed themselves flat against the building.

She watched Cade glance down the length of the house and study it. There were several windows along the rear, and a back door in the middle.

Cade moved forward, stopped at the first window, slowly leaning over to peer inside.

Five seconds later, he straightened, ducking and moving forward to the next window.

She understood immediately.

Nothing.

At the second, he leaned over again, only to quickly pull away. Piper's heart leapt, the urge to ask what he'd seen nearly unstoppable.

She managed to hold her tongue. A few seconds later, he repeated the motion, leaning in again, slower this time, to peer in the window.

He looked for what seemed like an eternity, before finally straightening. He glanced at her, his suddenly serious expression kicking her pulse up another notch.

He motioned her forward, gesturing with his thumb for her to look.

Nervous, terrified, Piper followed his lead, carefully approaching the window, then leaning over to look inside.

The room was dark. It took a moment for her

vision to adjust, for her to comprehend what she was seeing.

She stifled a gasp. A female figure sat in a chair, her arms tied behind her back, her ankles tied to the legs of the chair. She was blindfolded, her head was bowed, and the room was dark, but Piper didn't need a clear view to recognize her instantly.

Tara.

She looked so still that Piper felt a stab of fear deep within. She nearly pressed her face against the glass, desperate to see if Tara was even breathing.

It was too dark. She couldn't make out the figure that well.

She tried to tell herself Tara was simply asleep. It was the middle of the night. It was the most likely explanation.

Still, she needed to know for herself.

She had to get in that house.

Piper met Cade's eyes. Hard determination glittered in his, the sight reassuring. He knew what this meant to her, and was fully onboard.

They were getting Tara out of here.

The back door was a few feet away. Ducking below the window, they inched toward the entryway. Based on the rectangular window on the side of it, roughly the size as those found above a kitchen sink, Piper figured it opened on the kitchen.

Cade suddenly leaned closer, lowering his mouth to her ear. "Stay here," he said under his breath, the words barely audible. "I'm going to check the other windows, see if I can get a sense of how many people there are inside."

Of course. They couldn't just go in blindly. They needed to have some idea of who was in there, the situation they were heading into.

She watched him move silently to the edge of the house, checking the remaining windows, then slipping around the corner.

Gripping her Glock in front of her, she waited again, eyeing the shadows, listening for the slightest sound of movement in the house at her back. It was so late, and she doubted they were expecting intruders. She had to hope that meant there wouldn't be too many of them up and keeping watch, if any.

Cade finally reappeared, dodging around the corner and making his way back to her.

He held up two fingers, then pointed toward the front of the house.

She nodded her understanding. Two. There were two people in the front. At least that made things even.

Of course, at the slightest sign of trouble,

there were likely many more people in the house ready to wake and back up the two in the front of the house.

Best not to think about that and worry only about the immediate problem for the moment.

All that was left was to go in.

Even as she thought it, Cade reached for the knob. Meeting her eyes one more time, he gently turned it.

Piper fully expected they'd have to pick the lock. So she stared in disbelief as the knob turned in his hand, the latch releasing and the door sliding open a hair.

It was unlocked.

She supposed it made sense. They were in the middle of nowhere. The kidnappers were men with guns who probably figured they would hear anyone coming, if they actually did.

Evidently they weren't expecting a rancher and an accountant, she thought with grim satisfaction.

Using the tip of his rifle, Cade slowly began to ease the door open.

A squeal cut through the night air, as loud as a gunshot. One of the hinges, she guessed.

They both froze, waiting for the sound of raised voices, for lights to come on.

Piper was instantly torn about what to do if

the kidnappers did wake and come to see what was happening. Did she run? Her body rebelled at the possibility. No, she couldn't, not with Tara right there, so close. She couldn't leave her. It wasn't a possibility at all.

It took her several moments to register that no voices had sounded, no lights had come on.

The house remained as still and silent as it had been before.

Cade began to gradually push the door in farther again, until there was a gap just large enough for him to pass through.

He didn't though. He waited, then slowly leaned forward to give the room a quick scan.

It must have passed muster. Motioning for her to follow with a jerk of his shoulder, he slipped inside.

She followed moments later, on high alert. She'd been right. It was a kitchen. It was too dark to get many of the details.

The sound of a television from the front of the house, its volume turned down low, met their ears. She tensed, hoping someone had fallen asleep in front of it and wasn't currently watching it now. And certainly that they wouldn't end up wanting a midnight snack.

Either way she wasn't turning back, she thought, gripping her weapon tighter.

The room they'd seen Tara in appeared to be the first on the right, off the kitchen. Her eyes immediately sought out the hall that must lead to the room next to this one. Even as she spotted it, Cade was moving in that direction.

She zeroed in on the door immediately. As much as she wanted to rush to it and fling it open, Cade proceeded more carefully. He edged closer to the door, studying it around the edges. Searching for signs of an alarm, she realized. The hallway was dark, with only a little bit of light available to see anything, and she hoped that was enough. Cade couldn't exactly use his flashlight here, no matter how handy it would be.

Evidently satisfied, he crossed to the other side of the door then pressed himself against the wall. He gripped his rifle and motioned to her to be ready.

She nodded that she was, and quickly looked back down the hall toward the kitchen. She couldn't afford to let her guard waver at all.

Cade reached out and turned the doorknob. It opened in his hand. It was unlocked.

Once again, Piper could hardly believe it. But of course, the figure inside the room was tied up. They probably weren't worried about her getting away.

Still Cade eased open the door carefully. From the outside it hadn't looked like there was anyone in the room guarding her. But then, most of Piper's attention had been focused on the figure in the chair. Cade had taken a longer look, and she could only hope he was more certain.

She braced herself for the sound of an alarm or any kind of trap.

Nothing.

Cade created an opening, enough to look inside and dipped his head into the doorway. When he finally pulled back again, he nodded toward the room.

Piper hoped that meant the coast was clear. Either way, she stepped forward. Slipping inside, her attention immediately went to that same painfully still figure sitting in a chair in the center of what was largely an empty room.

Piper relived a moment's terror that something was wrong, that Tara was dead.

Before it could penetrate too deeply, the figure suddenly jerked up her head, as though sensing she wasn't alone, her body going stiff. Piper's heart leapt into her throat in sheer joy.

She was alive.

She was also scared as hell, Piper could tell, as Tara held herself utterly still.

Suddenly she started shaking her head, making muffled noises against the gag, struggling against her bindings.

Terrified someone would hear, Piper rushed over to her, taking her face in her hands and leaning close.

"Tara," she whispered. "It's me."

It took a second, but Tara stopped struggling and froze, her body tense with alertness.

"That's right," Piper murmured. "I'm going to get you out of here."

She tugged the blindfold loose so that Tara could see for herself that it was her. As soon as it was off, Tara blinked repeatedly, as though trying to clear her vision and adjust to the dark, her eyes searching the area around Piper. When her gaze finally landed, her shoulders slumped, tears filling her eyes.

Piper didn't lose any time untying the bindings on Tara's arms and legs. As soon as they were free, she helped Tara to her feet. Tara had barely made it upright when she threw her arms around Piper.

Piper gripped her just as tightly, tears burning her eyes. So many times over the past few days, she'd worried she'd never see Tara again. But here she was.

Tara was alive. She was here and whole and alive.

Then she felt Tara suddenly stiffen in her arms.

Alarmed, Piper pulled away. Tara was looking at something behind her, her eyes wide with fresh fear.

Piper jerked her head to see what Tara was looking at.

Relief shot through her.

Cade. It was just Cade. He stood at the door with his back to them. He was so big he did seem to fill the whole door.

"It's all right," Piper whispered. "He's a friend."

Tara relaxed only a fraction, never taking her eyes off him, her expression remaining wary. Piper could understand why her words might not completely combat the image he presented. He looked incredibly intimidating, that big figure cradling a rifle in his hands. Still, Tara allowed Piper to lead her toward the doorway, while clinging to Piper's arm as tightly as possible.

Cade didn't acknowledge them as they approached, his focus directed solely on what was happening outside the room. Only when they were a few feet away did he glance back at them. He looked long and hard at Tara for a moment, his gaze poring over her face as though seeking something. Piper didn't know whether or not he found it. He simply checked out the door again, then motioned them forward with a wave of his hand before stepping through himself.

Piper prodded Tara out first, so she would be between Piper and Cade. It was the safest place, which was exactly where she needed to be, especially since she wasn't armed. Once they were clear, Piper carefully pulled the door shut behind them.

They crept forward in a line, Piper never keeping her eyes in the same place, checking behind and around them, on full alert. They arrived at the kitchen, then the back door, without incident, slipping out into the night.

They made their way retracing their path, around the barn then into the darkness beyond. It seemed like a much longer distance than it had been getting there, probably because she was even more aware of the possibility of Tara's absence being discovered. With every step she expected to hear a shout from the building behind them, or even the sound of a weapon discharging.

Cade moved with absolute assurance, never

once hesitating or showing the slightest hint he didn't know where he was going. He never glanced back, but always seemed to sense when Tara's energy was flagging and the two of them had slowed, adjusting his speed accordingly.

They were seemingly in the middle of nowhere when Cade suddenly stopped and faced them.

"We need to hurry," Cade murmured under his breath, barely audible in the night air. Piper knew exactly what he meant.

It was time to run.

She looked at Tara. "Can you run?" Piper asked gently.

Tara considered the question for only a second before nodding vigorously, her jaw tightening with determination. The show of spirit sent fresh hope pouring through Piper's system. Whatever they'd done to her, they hadn't managed to kill Tara's fire.

Piper nodded and gave Tara's hand a small squeeze, then immediately lunged forward into the night. Tara fell into step alongside Piper, clutching her hand as though afraid Piper would let go.

They ran as fast as they could, Piper taking the lead, Cade falling behind them. She knew exactly what he was doing. He was keeping himself a bigger target, so if they were spotted and someone started shooting, it would be him they would be aiming at. She hated the idea of anything happening to him, and with every step braced herself for the sound of a gunshot or raised voices from the house behind them.

She heard nothing but the thudding of their footsteps on the dirt and her own heart pounding in her ears.

It started to seem as though they'd been running forever. It couldn't have taken this long to get to the house, even if they'd been walking. She started to fear she'd sent them in the wrong direction, though surely he would have corrected her. But if his attention was focused behind them…

Suddenly she saw the hazy figure of a horse up ahead, almost like a phantom in the night. Matt. The sight gave her a new burst of energy, and she picked up speed. Tara either saw it too or followed Piper's cue, because she accelerated at the same time without missing a step.

The horse gradually loomed larger, becoming two before long, and she saw the man standing in front of them, the rifle held in front of him. Matt.

When they reached him, Matt handed the

reins of Cade's horse to him, then turned to face Piper and Tara.

Piper felt Tara clutching her hand in a death grip and knew she had to be nervous about seeing another stranger.

"Tara, this is Matt," Piper said, gently leading Tara to Matt's side. "He's another friend. You'll ride with him, okay?"

Tara turned and gave a doubtful glance at Matt. He offered his hand to help her onto the horse. Tara hesitated for a moment, eyeing him warily, before placing her hand in his and allowing him to help her into the saddle.

As soon as Tara was off the ground, Piper hurried back to Cade, who was waiting by his horse. He helped her onto the horse's back, then quickly followed. He was barely in the saddle when he spurred the horse into motion. Piper looked to find Matt and Tara were already in motion beside them. Tara looked tense and shell-shocked, sitting stiffly in the circle of Matt's arms.

They moved slowly at first, just as they had on their approach in this area. Piper knew they had to, but every instinct in her body screamed to go faster, to get away as quickly as possible.

She sat tensely in Cade's arms, feeling the tightness in his own body all around her, and waited for the sound of gunfire, of raised voices, of someone coming after them.

An eternity later, with no warning, they must have reached the spot Cade and Matt thought was safe enough. The horses suddenly sprang into a run, spurred by whatever cue the men had given them.

Before she knew it, the horses were slowing again, and Piper saw the fence up ahead, illuminated in the moonlight. She held her breath the last few yards until they reached it, only exhaling once the men guided the horses through the fence and they were safely on the other side.

They stopped there. "Hold this," Cade suddenly said, his breath warm against her ear. "I'll be right back."

Before she could even think to respond, he was swinging himself out of the saddle and onto the ground. She watched him walk to the fence and she realized he was moving it back into place.

Piper glanced over at Tara to find her looking at her. Piper noticed Matt had released her slightly, his arms loose around her so he wasn't gripping her too tightly, as though recognizing how uncomfortable she must be, being held by a stranger and giving her as much space as he could. She would have given him a thankful glance, but his attention was focused off in the distance toward the house. Instead, Piper simply gave Tara a reassuring nod.

Then Cade was back, climbing up onto the horse behind her. Within moments, his arms were around her again, his fingers taking the reins from her hands. They began moving without a word, both horses proceeding forward in unison, starting at a walk then accelerating to a run.

Once again it passed in a blur. She was surrounded by the sound of hoofbeats, the western landscape stretching out around her, silvered by the moon.

And by Cade's arms about her, holding her close.

Then she spotted the lights of Cade's homestead up ahead, the sight sending fresh adrenaline through her.

As the house loomed larger in front of them, Piper only felt her excitement grow.

Then they were there.

The horses pulled to a stop in front of the house. The yard was as quiet as they'd left it, as though they'd never been gone at all when it seemed like they'd traveled for years.

She glanced into the darkness behind the

house, toward the ranch they'd just left, triumph and joy and relief surging within her.

Her gaze met Cade's eyes. His lips curved slightly and he nodded once. Gratitude burst in her chest for this man and everything he'd done. It was almost too much to believe.

They'd done it.

They were safe.

Chapter Nine

"You're sure I can't get you anything to eat?" Piper asked for what she knew had to be the hundredth time.

"I'm fine," Tara answered exactly as she had every time before. She sat on the edge of the bed in the room Cade had said she could use, right next to the one he'd given Piper. It was another kindness from a man she couldn't begin to thank for all he'd done.

Piper knew she was hovering, but she couldn't help it. She couldn't stop looking at her, couldn't stop wanting to do something for her. Even the fifteen minutes Tara had spent in the bathroom taking a shower and changing had seemed like an eternity. She looked better cleaned up, but sitting there, her hair still wet from the shower, her face tired and free of makeup, she also looked impossibly young. Matt had driven out to her rental car in the hours before they'd left for the Emerson ranch to exchange it for a new one, and retrieved Piper's suitcase, so at least Tara had something fresh to wear, but Piper's clothes seemed big on her. Just the thought of everything she'd been through in the past few days made Piper's heart ache.

"Do you want to talk about it?" she asked softly. She hadn't wanted to push, wanting to give Tara time to relax and get used to the idea that she was truly free.

Tara swallowed hard. "They were going to kill me," she whispered, keeping her head lowered. "Me and Pam, actually. When Pam came and gave them what they wanted, they were just going to kill us. They thought I couldn't understand them, because they were speaking Spanish to each other. They were just going to kill us. It was nothing to them. They didn't even care."

The horror and disbelief in Tara's voice filled Piper with fresh anger toward the men who'd put them through all of this. She wondered again who they were, who was behind it. The fact that the men had been speaking in Spanish was at least one clue.

"Did you hear them talking about anything else?" Piper asked, wanting as much to get Tara's mind off the topic as she wanted to learn what else Tara could tell her about the kidnappers.

"Not really. They left me alone most of the time, so I didn't get to hear too much. They weren't from here though. Most of them were from Mexico City, all of them from Mexico. I got that much."

Piper frowned. The man she'd been speaking with did have a slight accent. But why would a group of men from Mexico kidnap the sister of an FBI agent to force her to produce information from the FBI? "Did they say who they worked for?"

"No, they just referred to him as the boss. They were scared of him, I could tell that much."

If the man she'd been speaking with on the phone had been the boss, Piper could understand why they'd been scared of him. If it wasn't, and there was someone higher up, someone capable of intimidating the man on the phone... She nearly shuddered at the thought.

Instead, it was Tara who shuddered, pulling Piper out of her thoughts and back to her sister where they belonged.

"I really thought I was going to die," Tara said roughly, her head bowed. "No, I *knew* I was going to die. They thought they were going to kill us after Pam came and gave them what they wanted. Except I knew that Pam wasn't going to come. Pam wouldn't care that much, wouldn't risk her career by giving them information from the FBI, even for me. And when she didn't come, when they realized I wasn't somebody they could use to force her to do anything, they really would kill me. It was going to happen. My life was over."

Piper wanted to argue, wanted to tell Tara she was wrong. She knew where her younger sister was coming from. Pam never really had been there for her, for either of them. While Piper had compensated for their messed-up family life by taking over and trying to care for everybody, Pam had hardened, retreated into herself. She'd been gone most of Tara's teenage years, focused on her career, and neither Piper nor Tara had heard from her that often. But with Tara's life on the line, Pam obviously had been willing to do something, otherwise somebody wouldn't have gone to the trouble of trying to stop her.

Then Tara looked up and met Piper's gaze. "I should have known you'd come. You shouldn't have, but you did. You always do."

The gratitude and love on her sister's face

erased everything she'd been about to say. "Of course I do. You're my sister."

Tears rose in Tara's eyes. Piper felt her own burning, a lump lodging hard in her throat.

"Thank you," Tara said, her voice watery. "I love you, Piper."

"I love you, too, honey." She reached out and pulled Tara close. She knew she was probably holding on too tight, but couldn't help it, as Tara clung to her. She felt the sobs racking Tara's body, unable to stop the tears pouring down her own face. This was a moment she never thought she'd experience, yet here they were. Both alive, despite those men's intentions. Both safe.

They broke apart almost in unison. She watched as Tara swiped at her cheeks, finally unable to hold back the question that had been haunting her since this nightmare began. "Did they…hurt you?" she asked as gently as possible.

Tara shook her head. "No."

"Because you can tell me—"

Tara met her eyes with a look of annoyance Piper was all too familiar with, the flash of fire she saw easing her tension slightly. "They didn't do anything to me. At least not like that." The last few words drifted off, and Tara lowered her eyes again. "Some of them considered it, but the others told them the boss wouldn't like it. If I looked too roughed-up or traumatized when you came, you might decide not to cooperate and try to pull something that would jeopardize him getting the information he wanted."

Piper knew her sister well enough to believe she was telling the truth. She was thankful nothing had happened, but still couldn't feel much relief. The kidnappers may not have physically or sexually accosted her, but it was clear the experience of being taken, of spending all those days believing she was going to die, of being at the mercy of such terrible people, had understandably taken its toll on her.

Piper wished she could go back to the days when Tara was little and all it would take was a hug and a kissed boo-boo to make things all right again. If only this was the kind of hurt that could be so easily cured. But she knew it would take time, no matter how badly she wished she could take Tara's pain away.

She stroked a hand over Tara's hair. "It's over. You're safe now."

Tara gave a shaky nod, but didn't meet her eyes, and Piper knew she didn't believe her. After everything she'd been through, Piper couldn't blame her.

She pulled Tara close for another hug. After

a moment, some of the stiffness left Tara's body and she hugged her back, clinging tightly.

"Get some rest," Piper said. "I'll see you in the morning."

Tara started to pull away. Piper held on as long as she could, then finally released her.

Pushing off of the bed, Piper moved to the bedside table to turn off the lamp there.

"Leave it," Tara said when her hand was almost to it. "Please."

Piper glanced at her sister, who'd lain down on the bed. She was curled up on her side, not looking at Piper.

Her heart twisting, Piper nodded and dropped her hand. "All right. Good night."

Tara didn't respond. Piper headed to the doorway, stopping there for one last glance. Tara had closed her eyes but otherwise hadn't moved. Piper could tell she wasn't asleep yet, was probably waiting for Piper to leave so she could finally be alone and relax. Piper didn't want to go. All she wanted to do was stand there, drinking in the sight of her little sister, safe and secure, a sight she never thought she'd see again. For Tara's sake, she forced herself to step outside and gently pull the door shut behind her.

Swallowing a sigh, she made her way through

the empty house to the front, looking for Cade. Now that Tara was finally safe and Piper could catch her breath for the first time in days, she found herself really noticing the house. It was a big rambling structure, the kind of house made for a family, or at least the kind that should have one inside its walls. A far bigger house than was necessary for a man living alone.

The bedrooms she and Tara were in were sparse enough that Piper would bet they weren't occupied often, though they were done up so that they were ready for guests. She couldn't imagine Cade concerning himself with decorating or bothering to hire someone else to do it, but the rooms were organized well enough to suggest someone had gone to the trouble to do so, most likely a woman. Whoever that woman was, there was no indication she was still around. Piper couldn't help but wonder who that woman had been, why she wasn't here any longer.

As she moved past the living room, its lights still ablaze, she took it in, seeing the comfortable furniture, the lived-in atmosphere it presented. A big family might not live here, but it did very much feel like a home. The man who lived here had made it one for himself. She could imagine him sitting there at night, leaning back in the big comfortable chair with his feet propped up, watching the TV across from it or maybe reading a book, very much the king of his domain.

It was both a nice image, and also a little sad, picturing him alone. Or maybe not. For all she knew, he was happy being alone. She couldn't really guess how he felt, this man who'd done so much for her, yet whom she still knew so little about.

She found Cade on the front porch, standing with his back to her and staring out into the night. He didn't react to the soft squeal of the screen door opening and she hesitated in the doorway, suddenly uncertain. There was a rifle propped up against the porch railing at his side. He looked so vigilant, his shoulders broad, his attention unyielding, as though he were single-handedly capable of defending this house and everyone in it. It wouldn't have surprised her in the least if he could.

"Everything all right?" she asked softly.

He turned and looked at her. The moonlight slanted over the hard planes of his face, capturing every sharp angle and boldly masculine line, and she felt the breath hitch in her throat at the sight.

"No problems so far," he said. "Just keeping a lookout in case there are."

Piper nodded her understanding. When the kidnappers discovered that Tara was no longer there, they would move quickly to try and track where she'd gone. With any luck, it would be too difficult to do in the dark, but they couldn't count on that.

"How's your sister?" he asked.

"Okay, I guess. She's been through a lot, but I think she's going to be fine. She's tough."

His lips curved slightly at the sides. "Must run in the family."

Piper mustered a smile, but as she peered past him into the darkness, the expression quickly died.

"I lied to Tara," she admitted quietly. "I told her it's over, but it's not. They're not going to give up this easily. They were careless around her because they intended to kill her, and I have to consider the possibility they'll come after her to prevent her from identifying them in any way. I have to find out who's responsible and find some way to stop them."

"Don't worry. We will."

She frowned slightly in confusion, not sure how to take the words. It sounded as though he still intended to help her, though that hardly seemed necessary. She had Tara back. There was no reason to stay in the area, and every reason to leave as soon as possible. She would have considered doing so immediately if she had the energy to drive anywhere tonight. If anything, she would have thought he'd be glad to see her on her way.

Before she could comment, he continued, "Right now you need rest. You've earned it."

"You, too," she said. "You should get some sleep."

"I will in a little while."

She wondered if he was just saying that. Looking at him now, it was hard to believe he felt tired in the least, despite everything that had happened that day, everything he'd done.

Gratefulness swelled in her chest at the memory of all he'd risked for her, for Tara. She struggled to think of how to even begin to convey what she was feeling at this moment.

Finally, she simply said, "Thank you," the words seeming wholly insufficient for expressing her gratitude toward this man.

"You're welcome," he said roughly, the low, deep sound of those words sending a little shiver along her nerve endings.

There didn't seem to be anything left to say but good-night. Still she made no move to leave, feeling no particular need to do so. If he found anything odd about that, he didn't comment or make an attempt to see her on her way.

They stood looking at each other for a long moment, the silence gathering meaning the longer it went on, as though she could feel something heavy and palpable in the air between them.

He really was a very good-looking man, she thought, his features lean and masculine, his jaw square. A faint shadow of stubble dusted his cheeks, giving him an even more rugged look. His deep blue eyes seemed to stand out most of all. She could have stared into those eyes all night, seeking the answers to the mystery that was this man. Or maybe just to continue looking at the most attractive man she'd met in a while, as she felt tension building deep in her belly the longer she stood there.

It was more than just the way he looked that made him so appealing. It was the way he carried himself, that quiet confidence that said he knew who he was and was comfortable in his own skin. There was something so solid and straightforward about him, something that inspired confidence in her even though she seldom felt that way about anyone.

She didn't have to move her eyes to the rest

of him to know how big and strong he was. She still remembered keenly the feel of his arms around her, the solidness of his chest against her back as he'd held her tightly against him....

Suddenly he jerked his head around, breaking the spell.

Piper blinked in confusion, not understanding what had happened, why he'd so abruptly turned away.

Then she heard it, what he must have moments before.

The sound of an engine, that of a vehicle rapidly approaching on the main road to the ranch.

She followed his gaze to the road, her heart suddenly hammering for entirely different reasons than it had been moments earlier, instinct telling her who it must be.

It was as they'd thought.

The night wasn't over yet.

Chapter Ten

"Get back in the house," Cade ordered. *"Now."*

He didn't look to see if Piper did as he said, keeping his eyes firmly on the approaching vehicle. He automatically reached for the rifle propped up against the porch railing. She didn't say a word, and a moment later he didn't feel her presence behind him.

Matt was in the barn. Cade knew he would hear the new arrivals, and could offer backup even if he couldn't see him there. It would make sense for him not to make his presence known.

The truck had barely come to a stop when the doors were thrown open and the driver and two passengers climbed out. Two men seated in the bed jumped out of the sides and flanked the others, all five moving in unison, the driver in the lead as they approached the house. They were all Latino, not exactly a rare sight in New Mexico. It was still clear these men weren't locals and didn't really belong here. They were dressed like street toughs—tight T-shirts as though to show off their overblown muscles, dark jeans, combat boots—and gave off that feeling of danger.

"Can I help you gentlemen?" Cade called before they reached the steps. As he said it, he held the rifle loosely at his side, as though ready to raise it at any moment.

Which he damn well was.

The leader came to a stop a few feet from the steps, the others immediately halting behind him. All five men peered up at Cade, their expressions hard. Cade suspected he was supposed to feel intimidated. He didn't doubt they were armed but, at the moment, he was in a better position to swing up his firearm and open fire.

"Were you on our property tonight?" the leader demanded, his English lightly accented. Whoever he was, English wasn't his first language.

"I don't know who you are, so I couldn't say where your property is," Cade returned.

"It is the property next to yours to the east."

Cade furrowed his brow. "The old Emerson place? I've been wondering who bought that. Good to finally meet somebody from over there."

"Were you there tonight?" the man repeated with clear impatience.

"No, I wasn't."

"Someone came onto our property and stole something. It appears they entered from your property. We tracked footprints to the edge of our land, where there were fresh marks that horses had been there recently."

"I don't know what to tell you gentlemen. It wasn't me."

The man's expression tightened. "You are not here alone, are you? There are people who work for you? Maybe it was one of them."

"Everybody's asleep, and I know my people. None of them have any reason to go over to your property. More important, none of them would, especially without permission. If somebody sneaked onto your property, they could just as well have sneaked onto mine first."

"I think I would like to talk to your men," he said, the words sounding like an order. "Hear for myself."

The bastard had some nerve, Cade had to give him that. Showing up here with his posse was bad enough. Thinking he could get away with issuing orders to another man on the man's own property was something else altogether.

Cade tamped down his temper, not about to

lose his cool. "Like I said, everybody's asleep." He shrugged lightly. "Maybe the sheriff can sort this out. I already placed a call to him."

The man's eyes narrowed to slits. "Why would you do that?"

"He's a good friend of mine," Cade lied. "There's been talk of trouble in the area, thieves sneaking onto ranches, cattle rustlers, that sort of thing. I'm sure you must have heard of it. I don't often have visitors this late, so when I heard you coming, I figured I should give him a call in case it was trouble. He's on his way."

They stood there, locked in a silent standoff, neither moving, tension crackling in the air between them. Cade waited for the other man to retreat, fully prepared to stand there all night if necessary. There wasn't a chance in this world he was backing down.

The man caved first, exactly as Cade had known he would. He blinked, his gaze briefly flicking away. "I don't believe that is necessary," he said with barely concealed anger. "There must have been a mistake."

"Must have been," Cade agreed solemnly.

"Good night."

The men turned and started to move back to their truck when the leader suddenly stopped and glanced back at Cade. "'Trouble in the area,' huh? 'Thieves sneaking onto ranches'?"

"That's right."

The man just looked at Cade, a knowing, angry gleam in his eye. The man didn't believe him. Cade didn't really care, as long as he got the hell off his property.

"We are sorry to have bothered you," the man finally said, the words wholly insincere.

"No problem," Cade returned just as falsely.

He watched as the men climbed in their truck, each of them turning and looking back at him once they'd done so. He remained where he was until the truck's lights completely vanished and his unwanted visitors were gone.

He was about to pivot and enter the house when the door opened and Piper carefully stepped outside.

"Are you okay?"

He nodded. "Fine."

"I'm sorry. I shouldn't have just left you to face them alone like that."

"It's exactly what you should have done. The last thing we needed was for them to see you and know for sure that you're here."

"But they could have killed you, shot you down on the spot."

Something Cade was entirely too aware of.

Just thinking of the look in the leader's eyes when he'd stared him down, Cade had no doubt the man wouldn't have minded doing just that and storming the ranch until he found what he believed was here.

He shrugged, keeping his tone easy for her sake. "Don't worry about me. I can take care of myself. You have enough people to worry about—yourself included—to take me on, too."

He couldn't help but be strangely affected by her clear concern. He couldn't remember the last time anyone had looked at him with such obvious worry. He couldn't remember anyone ever doing it at all.

But then, he supposed he'd earned a bit of her loyalty by now, he thought dismissively. That was all it was, an extension of gratitude.

"We should leave," she murmured almost to herself.

He frowned. "What are you talking about?"

"Tara and I. We should get out of here."

"Where will you go?"

"I don't know. I'll figure it out. But you can't put yourself and Matt at risk any further."

"It's done. They clearly believe I helped you. Even if you leave, they'll still try to come over here if they want."

He saw her consider the words and finally

accept them, her shoulders slumping with resignation. "I'm sorry."

Hard to believe that less than twenty-four hours ago, he would have agreed with her. He had been unwilling to be pulled into this at first. But for her sake, he was glad he was.

"It's not your fault. And I'm not. You shouldn't have to deal with this on your own. Stay. You're safe here. They'll probably figure the last thing you'd do is stick around. We'll figure it out."

She looked up at him, her eyes searching his face as though trying to figure something out. He didn't know what. Then her expression eased, her mouth curving in a soft smile.

"Thank you."

The moonlight fell over her face, illuminating her features and giving her a kind of glow.

He'd known she was pretty, recognized that clear from the start. But in that moment, seeing her there, smiling up at him in the moonlight, it registered that she was downright beautiful.

He felt it again, the same tension building between them as it had earlier. He knew the instant she felt it too, her eyes widening slightly. She swallowed hard, her soft, supple lips parting slightly, her tongue darting out to wet them.

A jolt of heat shot straight to his groin at the sight.

He tried to tell himself his reaction wasn't about her. It had been a while since he'd been with a woman. He'd be reacting this way around any woman. It wasn't her specifically.

He knew he was kidding himself. He knew what it felt like to be attracted to a woman, what simple arousal felt like. This was something else. He was attracted to her, sure. But that didn't account for the heaviness he felt in his chest, or just how that smile affected him.

The instinct was there to move forward, to remove the distance between them, to touch her. He'd already done it tonight, when he'd lifted her onto the horse, when he'd had her in his arms on their way to and from the Emerson ranch house. He knew how soft she felt, and wanted nothing more than to feel it again.

Which would be a mistake, of course. For both of them.

He made himself nod. "Good night."

"Night," she said softly, the sound of her voice a caress against his skin. He nearly shuddered.

He watched her step into the house, the screen door closing gently behind her. His gaze remained on the empty doorway far too long after she'd gone. He couldn't move away.

The sound of footsteps hitting dirt drew his attention to his left.

Matt stood there, having approached the front of the house unnoticed, looking up at him. He didn't say anything. He simply gave Cade a look that communicated more than enough. It wasn't anger, or disappointment. It was worse.

It was pity.

Cade tried to glare back at him, wanted to communicate just as clearly that his friend was wrong.

But as his mind returned to the woman who'd just gone inside, a woman unlike any he'd ever met, a woman he liked far too much for somebody he'd known for less than a day, he knew with a sick feeling in his gut that Matt wasn't wrong at all.

Chapter Eleven

Something was wrong.

The flash of intuition disturbed Castillo's thoughts, and he raised his head, his frown deepening. He realized that something had been nudging at his subconscious for a while, only now becoming strong enough to break through to the surface.

It was just after eight o'clock, but he'd been awake for some time, unable to sleep. He couldn't remember when he'd last slept for more than a few hours. Thoughts of Ricardo weighed too heavily on his mind, as they always did. That was even more the case now that he was so close to finally achieving justice. He was not the young man he'd once been, and there were times he'd never felt more tired. But the righteousness of his mission gave him the energy he needed and drove him onward.

This morning there were plans he needed to be making, arrangements for the next meeting with Pamela Lowry. Still, something had distracted him. He looked at the door, eyes narrowing as he considered what it was that bothered him.

The quiet—that was it. The house was quiet. Too quiet. Yes, it was early, but still, the house was far quieter than it should be.

He listened carefully. It wasn't that the house was empty or that most were still asleep. No, he could feel it—the tension—the nervous energy—in the air, filling the house. It was as if they were keeping their voices lowered, conversations being held in hushed breaths to keep them secret.

Something had happened. Something that wasn't good.

Something he suspected his men didn't want to tell him about.

Something they'd damn well better.

He waited, tension coiling in the pit of his stomach at the thought that his men were trying to keep something from him. Diaz would know better. Because if Castillo had to go out there and ask what was wrong, his wrath over whatever they might have done would only be greater.

The knock came when his irritation was near

its breaking point. He didn't relax a bit, simply calling out, "Enter."

The door opened slightly, and Diaz poked his head in. "I'm sorry to disturb you—"

"What is it?"

His expression carefully blank, Diaz stepped fully through the gap, closing the door behind him and squaring his shoulders to face Castillo directly. "The girl is missing."

It took a moment for him to process the words. They made so little sense. "How?"

Diaz's jaw tightened, the only sign of his frustration. Or fear? "We don't know. Ortega checked on her at three o'clock and she was gone—"

"Three o'clock, and you are only telling me now?"

The color that appeared in Diaz's dark cheeks indicated he knew what a mistake that had been. "I didn't want to bother you unnecessarily, and we were conducting a search of the grounds."

"And you found her."

"No."

"You searched everywhere?"

"Yes."

"She must have had help. She couldn't have

gotten away by herself. One of the men?" he wondered aloud.

Diaz shook his head. "All are accounted for. And none of them would have."

No, of course not, Castillo thought, already answering his own question. Even if one of them did harbor that kind of sympathy for the girl, they all knew better than to cross him. There was only one person who would do that for the girl's sake.

It was the sister, of course. Who else?

Rage exploded through his body, the heat of it searing through him, blinding him, nearly making him scream, the fury almost incapable of being contained.

He'd underestimated her. She may only be a woman, she may have just been in a car accident, but Pamela Lowry was an FBI agent. Of course she would try to attempt a rescue. He didn't know how she'd determined their location—the ranch was registered under a shell corporation that couldn't be traced back to him—but he should have considered the possibility she might, thought about the resources she had at her disposal. A mistake, and he alone was to blame.

It was as he'd thought—she would do whatever she had to for her family. Under different circumstances he might have respected it.

These were not those circumstances.

She would pay for this. Now Ricardo's killer wasn't the only one who would be punished. Before this she and her sister would have died simply, quickly. No longer. For this she would suffer. He would find them—he had no doubt of that—and they would pay harshly.

He listened as Diaz described the men's late-night visit to the ranch next door. Yes, it did seem likely that Pamela Lowry had escaped with her sister by traveling onto the other ranch, whether or not it was with the help of the people over there. Either way, it was unlikely the women were still there. They probably would have wasted little time getting as far away from here as possible—taking the name of Ricardo's killer with them.

They could run, but they would be found. In the meantime, though...

Despair washed over him, agony gripping his insides and nearly buckling his knees. *No.*

He'd been so close. Ricardo had nearly had justice, and now he had to start over again, to learn the name of his son's killer, to see the bastard pay—

And then he noticed Diaz had not moved, that

blank expression still on his face, and he realized there was more.

He said nothing, simply waited for Diaz to continue.

The man finally, reluctantly, began to speak.

Castillo listened intently, the words that met his ears filling him with fresh rage.

Idiots. He was surrounded by idiots. Stupid, incompetent idiots.

He was on the verge of giving vent to his fury when the information sank in, stilling his tongue. As he considered the implications, he relaxed, excitement beginning to stir in his gut instead.

No, this wasn't bad news. It was an opportunity, a gift that had been dropped in his lap just when he needed it.

And he was a man who firmly believed in using every opportunity to his advantage.

WHEN SHE FINALLY GOT TO BED, Piper expected to practically sleep the day away. By the time she crawled beneath the covers, the weariness seemed to have settled into every cell of her body, weighing down on her until she could barely move. Despite her nap yesterday, it felt as though she hadn't slept in weeks. But when she woke up, it wasn't even noon.

She lay there for a while, sensing she wouldn't

be able to fall back to sleep. Despite getting less than six hours, she felt completely rested. Maybe it was because she'd slept soundly enough in those six hours that she hadn't needed any more. Maybe it was because, for the first time in a very long while, she'd dreamed—good dreams that had made for a pleasant night's rest.

Or maybe it had been what she'd been dreaming about.

A tremor quaked through her at the memory. Cade. She'd dreamed of Cade.

It was strange and ridiculous and so many other things. She couldn't remember the last time she'd dreamed of a man, let alone one she barely knew. Yet there he'd been, as he'd looked the first time she'd met him, climbing out of his truck and striding toward her. As he'd looked in his living room, his face softened with sympathy and concern. As he'd looked reaching for her when she'd been on the horse, strong and sure, ready to help her down. As he'd looked standing on the porch in the moonlight, staring out into the dark, his broad shoulders offering a reassuring barrier against the rest of the world.

Or staring down at her, his eyes dark with an emotion that sent a thrill through her just remembering it.

It wasn't hard to understand why the man had

infiltrated her subconscious so thoroughly. He was like no other she'd ever met before. Strong and kind. Reserved, yet caring. Noble, but modest, wanting no credit or praise for doing things that went far beyond what could reasonably be expected of anyone.

With everything that had happened and everything yet to be resolved, there should be more important things on her mind. But after the past few days, she was grateful her subconscious had reached for something more pleasant to contemplate in her dreams.

Unfortunately, she'd gotten all the sleep she was going to. Realizing there were things she should be doing, Piper got up and dressed quickly.

She was about to leave the room when she glanced back and saw the cell phone she'd left on the bedside table. She knew the kidnapper hadn't called. She would have heard the phone ring. Still, she suspected it was only a matter of time before the kidnapper was in touch. She knew better than to think last night had been the end of it. Frankly she was surprised those men hadn't come back after a while. They probably could have seen that the authorities hadn't come, and they had to suspect she was here. Why hadn't they made another move?

Whatever the reason, she should take the phone. She had no idea what she would say to the kidnapper if he called. Apparently she would find out when the moment came. Retrieving the phone, she shoved it in her pocket and headed out of the room.

She checked on Tara, who she was relieved to find still asleep. Staying in the doorway of the room, she studied her sister. Tara's expression was more relaxed in slumber, but she was still curled up on her side, her posture defensive. She looked so vulnerable it was all Piper could do not to crawl in beside her and throw her arms around her, but she didn't want to disturb Tara's much needed rest. She made herself close the door again and head to the kitchen.

Stepping inside, Piper found Matt standing at the counter with his back to her, pouring himself a cup of coffee.

She hesitated, not sure if she was up to facing the man yet this morning. Before she could decide what to do, he turned and spotted her. He eyed her over the rim of the coffee mug. It was a look she couldn't quite decipher, not uncomfortable exactly, more contemplative, as though he was trying to figure her out. She couldn't imagine why. If anything, her life seemed far too much of an open book to this man.

"Don't you ever sleep?" she asked, moving farther into the kitchen and trying for an easy tone.

"Too much going on around here to make it easy to get any sleep."

She grimaced. "I'm sorry you got pulled into this. I never intended for anyone else to get dragged into this situation."

"I know," he said simply, with enough sincerity she was surprised. "It's not your fault."

Her thoughts must have been written across her face, because he continued, "You look surprised."

"To be honest, I am," she admitted. "I thought you didn't like me."

"It's not you," he said. "Cade just can't help himself when he sees a woman in trouble."

"He's helped other women in trouble?"

"Not since Caitlin."

"Who's Caitlin?" Piper asked without thinking.

She could tell immediately Matt thought he'd said too much, his eyes sliding away for a moment. Then without looking back at her, he said into his coffee mug, "Cade's ex-wife."

"Oh." This time there was no reason for her

to be surprised. Cade was a man in his late thirties. She'd been surprised that he wasn't married. It made sense that he would have been once. A million questions immediately came to mind all at once. The one that came out was, "She was in trouble when they met?"

A pained expression on his face, Matt gave his head a sharp shake. "It's not really my place to say anything. I shouldn't have said that much. Excuse me."

Without looking at her, he quickly turned and walked out the back door, leaving her alone in the room.

Piper slowly crossed to the counter and reached for the coffeepot to pour herself a cup. She couldn't help wondering about the woman Cade had married. Where was she now? What had happened between them? What kind of woman was Cade McClain attracted to?

Why did it even matter to her?

The last question was the most troubling, and the one that nagged at her as she sank onto a stool at the counter to drink her coffee.

She was still mulling it over when Cade entered the room.

At the sight of him, she felt a ridiculous surge of emotion rise from the pit of her stomach, something that felt an awful lot like anticipation, even excitement. Of course, given the view he presented, it was hard not to get excited. He looked as good in the light of day as he had in her dreams. He was wearing a button-down shirt tucked into his jeans, the garment emphasizing the broadness of his shoulders, the solidness of his chest, the flatness of his belly. The jeans were faded and well-worn, molding to his strong thighs as he strode across the room. Watching the fabric shift and cling to his legs with every movement, she wondered idly if the view was as good from behind.

As soon as she realized what she was doing, she blinked and raised her gaze. Sure, the man was good-looking, but she had to get a grip. She had other things she should focus on, and he certainly didn't need to see her checking him out.

Fortunately he didn't appear to have noticed her. He moved toward the counter almost absentmindedly, his head slightly bent, his brow furrowed as though he was deep in thought. Even with the pensive expression on it, his was an undeniably handsome face. Of course a man like him—an apparently successful rancher and landowner, a kind, good man, and an incredibly fine male specimen at that—would have been married. Who was this woman who'd let him go? Or had he let her go, and why?

It was only when he was nearly to the counter that he looked up and spotted her. She automatically began to muster a smile, preparing to say good morning. Something in the look on his face killed the response, and the smile died on her lips. His expression was cautious, almost wary as he eyed her for a moment before turning toward the counter.

"Good morning," he murmured.

"Morning," she echoed, trying to decipher what she thought she'd seen.

"How's your sister?" he asked as he reached for the coffeepot.

"Still sleeping."

"I'm sure she can use it. Same goes for you. Why are you up already?"

"Got all the sleep I needed, I guess. I still have too much to do."

"Any thoughts on that front?"

"We can start by checking online. We may be able to find something there."

"Good idea. I have a computer in my office. You can use it. Do you want something to eat?"

She shook her head. "I'm not hungry. I can wait while you make something for yourself though."

"Nah, I'm good. Grabbed something before I headed to bed this morning."

"What about the people who work for you? Do you need to make something for them?"

"I gave everybody a few days off. I don't want them getting caught up in any of this. They're safer staying away for a while."

"Of course," Piper murmured. She couldn't help but feel a little guilty. She almost asked if he was going to pay them for the lost days, or wondered if she should offer to. But she had no idea how much that would be, or if it was even any of her business. Either way, it was a reminder that there were other people counting on this situation being resolved as soon as possible.

Picking up the cup of coffee he poured for himself, Cade motioned toward the hallway with his shoulder. "Come with me."

She followed him into the hall. He walked to the end and pushed the last door open. As soon as he glanced inside, he swore under his breath and hurried in.

Curious what had caused the reaction, she moved into the doorway and peered into the room.

There was paper everywhere, both ledgers and loose sheets, spread out on the desk, piled up on the floor, stacked on a nearby table. She couldn't see a single clear surface anywhere.

He began gathering the papers on the desk into a pile. "Sorry about the mess. I've been going over the books. Tax season isn't that far off."

She resisted the urge to say it looked like he shouldn't be doing his own books. "Do you need some help?" she asked tactfully. "I'm an accountant. I can take a look at them if you want."

He started moving paper to the nearby table that already had plenty on it. "I appreciate the offer, but I'm pretty sure you have more important things to think about right now."

He was right. She did. Still, she wouldn't have minded helping him. It looked like he could use it, and it was certainly the least she could do. Maybe after all this was done...

She nearly shook her head. What was she thinking? She would be leaving as soon as all of this was over. She'd disrupted his life and that of everyone on the ranch more than enough as it was. He certainly wouldn't want her sticking around any longer than was absolutely necessary.

But as she remembered the way he'd looked

at her last night on the porch, she could almost imagine that wasn't necessarily true.

He suddenly sat down at the desk and she realized he had most of the paper cleared, enough that they had some room to work. He turned on the computer and it started to boot. "So an accountant, huh? Do you like doing that?"

"I like numbers, always have. It pays well and I'm good at it. It's not the most exciting job, that's for sure. You might not think so based on the past few days, but my life is usually pretty boring."

"Is that why you had no trouble risking it?"

She cocked her head and studied him. "You still don't approve of my plan yesterday, do you?"

"Willingly getting yourself killed doesn't sound like much of a plan to me," he muttered.

"Even to save a loved one? You said it yourself, Tara is more like my daughter than my sister."

"Right."

"You find that hard to believe."

"No, I believe you."

"You just don't understand it. I remember."

"Guess I just never experienced that kind of parental devotion myself," he murmured.

She frowned at the admission. Her curiosity was naturally piqued, but she didn't want to pry.

He glanced up and caught her expression. Grimacing, he said, "My parents weren't much better than your mother."

"Oh?"

He shrugged. "When my mother got pregnant, my father did what he was supposed to and married her, and resented the hell out of the both of us for the rest of his life. My mother took off when I was seven."

"I'm sorry. I know how tough that must have been."

Another shrug. "I survived."

"What about you? You really never had anybody you loved that much?"

"Thought I did. Good thing I never had to prove it, because it turned out she wasn't worth it."

"Your ex-wife," Piper said, more a conclusion than a question.

Surprise flashed across his face. "How did you—" He grimaced, anger replacing the surprise. "Matt."

"He didn't say much about her," she said quickly. "Just that you had an ex-wife and you helped her when she was in trouble."

"That about covers it."

"I have a feeling there's a lot more to the story," she confirmed.

"Why do you want to know?"

"I guess I'm still trying to figure you out. You risked your life for me and Tara. Why?"

He glanced away, looking distinctly uncomfortable. "Somebody—"

"Had to," she finished for him. "Except they didn't. Most people wouldn't have. You didn't have to. But you did. Why?"

A wry grin touched his lips. "It wasn't love, if that's what you're thinking."

She matched his grin, the very thought ridiculous. He hadn't even known her, which just made it all the more remarkable. "Of course not. So what was it? Goodness? Kindness?" *Because you can't resist helping a woman in trouble?*

He simply nodded at the computer. "It's up and running," he said, rising from the chair and rounding the opposite side of the desk. "You're good to go."

She didn't miss the fact that he was deliberately avoiding answering her question. Part of her was tempted to press for an answer, but she thought better of it. Whatever his reasons, she didn't want to do anything to make him regret his decisions.

"All right then," she said. "Let's get to work."

Moving behind the desk, she lowered herself into the chair. He'd already opened a browser window and left it up on the screen.

"I guess the easiest thing to do would be a general search for news articles about the FBI in Dallas," Piper said, automatically entering the terms in the search box.

It didn't take her long to find something. "This is interesting," she said after reading a few articles that had come up.

He looked up from the papers he'd been going through on a nearby table. "What is it?"

"The biggest story involving the FBI in the past year appears to be a raid on a massive identity theft operation nine months ago. During the raid, the suspected ringleader, a man named Ricardo Castillo, was killed. All the agents involved, none of whom were named, were exonerated in the shooting. And here's something—Ricardo was the son of Esteban Castillo, a notorious Mexican crime boss."

"Who naturally wouldn't have been happy with his son's death and might be out for revenge," Cade concluded.

"Which explains why the men who were holding Tara came from Mexico." She suddenly realized she hadn't told him that and glanced up from the monitor to find him looking at her, a question in his eyes. "Tara studied Spanish all through high school and now in college. She said the men spoke Spanish, and managed to catch that most of them were from Mexico City."

"Then it certainly adds up," he agreed.

"It also could explain why they targeted Pam. She's been in the Dallas office less than six months, which means she wasn't involved in the shooting, but would still be able to access the names of those who were."

"What else can you find out about this Castillo?" he asked, moving to stand behind her so he could see the screen.

She quickly did another search. It brought up numerous results, many of them in Spanish from Mexican news sources. Piper read a half dozen of the ones in English, Cade reading over her shoulder. With every word, she felt her heart sinking lower and lower.

Esteban Castillo was reputed to be rich, ruthless, incredibly dangerous and virtually untouchable. Though he had a number of legitimate businesses, he'd been connected to more than two dozen criminal enterprises, including drugs, weapons and human trafficking, but had never faced justice, despite being believed to be

connected to numerous deaths. With a father
like him, it was probably no wonder his son had
also wound up following a life of crime.

"If this Esteban Castillo is behind this, we
may be in even more trouble than I thought,"
she said. "Who knows what kind of resources
a man like that probably has?"

"With his kind of money, I'd say limitless,"
Cade replied, sounding no more happy about
it than she was. He had to be wondering what
exactly it was she'd gotten him into. First cor-
rupt FBI agents, now this? Heck, she still
couldn't believe *she* was involved in this.

Even more important, how could they possibly stand a chance against a man like that?

A piercing trill suddenly disrupted the silence that had fallen over the room. Piper nearly
jumped out of her skin, and felt Cade react
behind her.

She reached down and fished the offending
object out of her pocket.

The cell phone.

It was the kidnapper.

Chapter Twelve

Piper lifted the phone with trembling fingers and forced herself to answer the call. "Hello?"

"I presume this is *Piper* Lowry I am speaking to?"

The voice was exactly what she expected, but the question caught her so off guard Piper was shocked into silence.

Which, of course, was answer enough. "I thought so," the man said with a trace of barely controlled anger. "Pamela Lowry has been in a coma for four days following a car accident. It was careless of someone to see you and simply assume you were her without checking further. The person who made that mistake has been dealt with."

A shudder ran through her at the coldness in the words. Piper had no doubt exactly how that person had been "dealt with."

Trying her best not to feel intimidated by the

man and his insinuations, Piper forced herself to speak. "All right, so you know. Now what?"

"Now you and I will make a new deal."

"Why would I make any kind of deal with you?"

"Because you may have taken your younger sister from my men, and I have no doubt it was you—" this time his anger sounded on the verge of breaking through "—but your sister Pamela is hardly safe, is she?"

Piper's heart stopped. "What are you talking about?" she whispered.

"She's simply lying there, helpless, unable to defend herself. Hospitals aren't very secure places, are they? Nearly anyone can get in and out, enter rooms they shouldn't be in. Someone may even be there now."

Oh, God.

She'd saved one sister, only to have the man turn around and use the other as a pawn.

She should have thought of this, should have known the man would figure this out, should have seen how Pam could be used this way. Why hadn't she? The image of Pam, exactly as the man had described, rose in her mind. She was completely helpless, could not fend off any kind of attack, and Piper was hundreds of miles away, just as useless to protect her.

"Why are you doing this?" she asked, trying to keep her voice from shaking as the image refused to fade.

"You will still provide me with what I want."

"The names of the agents involved in the raid that resulted in the death of Ricardo Castillo."

This time it was he who fell into a surprised silence, Piper noted with no small satisfaction.

"Very good, Miss Lowry. Now you need only to get me those names."

"I'm not with the FBI. How am I supposed to get that information?"

"I'm certain you will find a way. You seem to be a very resourceful woman, Miss Lowry, and very good at getting information. Otherwise there's no reason for me to allow your sister Pamela to live."

"There's no reason to kill her, either! She hasn't done anything to you. None of us has!"

"*You* did, Miss Lowry. You lied to me about who you were. You lied to me about having the information I require. You broke onto my property last night. You made fools of my men. We had an arrangement, one which *you* violated. Did you really think I wouldn't respond to you taking your sister back?"

No, of course she hadn't, though she could hardly admit that to him. She simply hadn't imagined just how much worse things could get again. "So what happens now?"

"Get the names of the agents. That's all I want. I will be in touch."

The call was disconnected, leaving Piper with nothing to do but lower the phone she barely seemed capable of holding on to with fingers that had gone numb.

"What is it?" Cade asked, concern heavy in his voice.

"It really isn't over."

"What did he say?" Cade demanded.

"He knows I'm not Pam, that she's in the hospital, and he still wants the names of the agents involved in the death of Ricardo Castillo."

"Damn," he muttered. "That doesn't make any sense. How can he expect you to get that?"

"I'm not sure he does. I think he's angry I fooled him and was able to get Tara back and just wants revenge at this point, the same way he does against the agent or agents who'd killed Ricardo." Just remembering the edge in the man's voice was nearly enough to make her shudder. "He's giving me a chance to get the information, just in case there is some way I can deliver and he can get out of this with what he wanted all along. But I don't believe for a second that will be the end of it, and stop him from wanting to punish me somehow."

"He can want whatever he likes. It's not going to happen."

The fierceness in the words left no doubt he meant every one and she couldn't help giving him a small smile, warmth gathering in her chest. He was so big and forceful it really did seem as though he was capable of fending off Castillo and his forces entirely on his own.

Meeting her eyes, he gave her a sharp nod, his expression utterly serious, as though confirming his vow. The absolute solemnity in his gaze made her melt a little more inside, and she was reminded how lucky she was to have found this man and have him on her side.

She'd never thought she needed anyone to fight her battles, had never had anyone who was willing to even try. She had to admit that it felt good having this man with her through this ordeal.

Except Pam didn't have anyone on her side, she remembered, instantly sobering. She was all alone, completely vulnerable to attack.

"There's something else I should have realized," she said. "The kidnappers aren't the only threat to Pam. Whoever's responsible for her accident—maybe the FBI agents she cannot trust—also have reason to try to finish her off while she's unconscious. She probably knows who would try to hurt her, or at least could figure it out once she wakes up, so they would need to prevent her from waking up at all. If they hadn't been so busy trying to stop me, they might have already done so." Her heart stopped. "If they haven't already. I have to call the hospital."

"Good idea. Tell them you have reason to believe she's in danger and they may be able to put extra security on her room. At least it's something."

Something, she agreed as she started dialing. She just had to hope it was enough.

It took her a few minutes to get in touch with someone on Pam's floor, every second she waited feeling like an eternity.

A nurse finally came on the line. Piper quickly identified herself and asked for a status update.

"I'm afraid her condition hasn't changed. She's still stable, but hasn't regained consciousness."

"Has anyone checked on her recently?"

Piper could tell from the woman's silence she'd caught her off guard. "I was just in there about ten minutes ago."

"And nothing's happened to her?"

"No," the woman said slowly. "Like I said, her condition hasn't changed." A beat. "Is everything all right, Ms. Lowry?"

"I hope so. I don't know if you're aware, but my sister is an FBI agent and there's reason to believe her life is in danger. Is there any way to increase security on her room?"

"Of course, I can certainly have security check on her as often as possible, but I don't know if they have enough people to post someone on the room full-time. If she's with the FBI, wouldn't they be better equipped to handle that?"

Piper swallowed a sigh. "Of course they are," she agreed since she could hardly explain the circumstances to this woman. "I've been in touch with Pam's boss and he assured me they'll send someone shortly, but if you could have someone check on her in the meantime, I'd appreciate it."

"I can certainly do that."

Piper thanked the woman for her help and hung up the phone, not in the least reassured by the conversation. "She's okay for the moment, but just because nothing's happened to her yet doesn't mean it still couldn't. I should hire private security or something to watch over her, but I can't afford anything like that."

"She should be fine for the time being. Just like Tara, they're not going to hurt her as long as they can use her to possibly get what they want."

"That's true for the kidnappers, but what about the person with the FBI? Even if hospital security does check on Pam, all that person would have to do is show his or her FBI credentials to get access to her and finish her off."

"That person's not going to risk being identified as going into her room if something happens to her. Besides, I doubt that person is even in Dallas right now. He's probably a little busy at the moment trying to track you down, or is gone entirely if he thinks you've already given Castillo his name. Pam's no threat to reveal anything right now, but this person seems to think you have something—probably this information for Castillo—which means you have to be stopped."

The reminder that there was someone out there searching for her, someone who likely wanted to kill her immediately, not toy with her like Castillo, should have filled her with dread. It did a little, but mostly it was reassuring, exactly as he'd intended. She would much rather have the threat be against herself—she could defend herself—than Pam, who couldn't.

"I hope you're right."

"This bastard's not going to win," he said firmly. "None of them are. We just have to figure out a way to stop them."

He was right of course. That was exactly what they had to do. She let his words and his certainty settle into her bones, washing away her fear, leaving determination in its wake.

She blinked up at him, ready to thank him for being there, for reassuring her again. He really was remarkable. That a man as big and masculine and commanding as he was could be so kind and considerate still amazed her. With his combination of strength and courage and decency, all of it shining in his deep blue eyes—

Eyes she was staring into, she realized with a start.

Only then did it hit her how close they were, how near to each other they'd moved as they were speaking without her noticing it. Even closer than they'd been last night.

And she was just standing there, staring up into his eyes without saying a word.

And he was staring back.

Adrenaline shot through her at the knowledge. Yes, he was just standing there, too, inches away, looking back at her.

She saw the instant he realized it, as well, his fierce expression fading slightly, his eyes darkening.

Then she felt it, the same tension she'd felt between them last night, what she'd remembered in her dreams, now too tangible to be mistaken for anything but what it was.

Attraction. Chemistry.

Something more potent than anything she'd felt in a long time, if ever. Maybe because he was unlike any other....

She gave herself a little shake. It didn't matter what it was. This wasn't the time for it.

She thought of Pam, of Tara, of the situation still weighing down on them all, and wondered what she was doing. God, if he even knew what she was thinking, he would probably believe she was an idiot.

Even as she considered it, she found herself looking back into his incredibly blue eyes and that ruggedly masculine face, and something told her that wasn't what he was thinking at all.

She cleared her throat, forcing her gaze away from him. "Tara might be up by now. I should check on her."

"Right," he said roughly, stepping back.

She hurried from the room, drawing a breath as soon as she was through the doorway.

She really hadn't ever met a man like him before. She was grateful she had now, but only for the help that he was giving her and everything he was doing for them. It was all she could begin to consider.

If only she didn't seem to be having so much trouble remembering that.

Chapter Thirteen

Two hours later, Piper should have been feeling better. Tara had indeed been up by the time Piper left the office, and they'd had lunch together. Tara seemed a lot better this morning, well rested and more relaxed, as she was finally able to start letting go of the ordeal she'd experienced.

Piper only wished she could relax, but she couldn't. Because she still didn't have a way out of this mess.

She'd tried to keep a calm front while talking to Tara, but inside her tension had built by the minute, her mind constantly turning without ever landing on the solution they desperately needed.

Finally when Tara excused herself, Piper turned to Cade, unable to deny the conclusion she'd been forced to reach. "I think we've gone as far as we can on our own. We need help with this. Somehow we have to figure out who we can trust."

"Finally ready to call in the local authorities?"

She shook her head. "No. I'm still not sure they can be trusted. I need to figure out who Pam was close to. Maybe I can narrow down who she probably would have spoken to that she shouldn't have, and who I can talk to now." Not for the first time, she wished she and Pam had been closer. If they somehow managed to get out of this mess alive and well, she vowed she wouldn't let her sister remain a stranger to her.

"Any ideas how to do that?" Cade asked.

"I suppose if I went back to her apartment in Dallas, I could try to find her address book or access her computer...." The answer came to her in a flash, sending her bolting upright in her seat. "Her email."

"What do you mean?"

"Pam had a personal email account outside her official FBI one. If I can access it, maybe I can see who she corresponded with the most, maybe see what she said to them in her messages and vice versa to get a sense of who they were to her."

"Do you know her password?"

"No, but I know her address and I use the same service she does. I know that when you forget your password, they ask you security questions in order to access your account, and with any luck, I'll know Pam well enough to be able to answer those questions." She and Pam may not have been close, but she bet she still knew her better than most.

They quickly made their way back to his office. Pulling up the login page for the email service, Piper typed in Pam's email address, then clicked the link to say she'd lost her password. As expected, the form notified her that to change her password and access her account, she would have to answer several security questions which she had previously answered when she opened the account. Drawing in a breath, Piper read the first question.

What was the name of your first boyfriend/ girlfriend?

Easy, Piper thought. Billy Conroy. Pam had been crazy about him.

What street did you grow up on?

Applegate.

What was the name of your first pet?

Trick question. Leave it to Pam to pick a question that didn't have an answer. They'd never had one growing up, and Piper knew

Pam's career kept her too busy to care for a pet, unless she'd gotten a goldfish.

Hoping she hadn't, Piper typed in "None," then clicked to confirm she'd answered all the questions.

A moment later Pam's Inbox appeared on the screen.

Triumph surged within her, just as Cade said, "You did it," and leaned closer.

For an instant, the breakthrough was forgotten, overwhelmed by his sudden closeness. He wasn't touching her. It didn't matter. She could still feel him as palpably as if he was, his sheer heat warming her skin. She inhaled sharply, only realizing after she'd done so that she'd drawn the scent of him straight into her system. He wasn't wearing any cologne or aftershave. No, the scent she detected was all him, pure, heady maleness.

She didn't think she'd ever smelled anything better.

She blinked. God, what was happening to her?

"What's that?" Cade asked.

She managed to focus on the screen to see the message he was pointing at, immediately seeing what had caught his attention, what should have caught hers. "It looks like a message Pam sent to herself," she murmured, clicking on it.

The email didn't contain a message, just an attached file. Piper automatically clicked to open it.

It took her a moment to realize what she was reading.

"Is this...?" Cade asked over her shoulder, his tone reflecting the same astonishment she was feeling.

"It looks like the file on the shooting of Ricardo Castillo," Piper said. Part of her was shocked to see it. This was a classified FBI file. Pam had broken the law to obtain it, all to save Tara's life. Sure, she herself had been willing to sacrifice to save Tara, but Pam's career meant so much to her, and there were times over the years Piper had had the same doubts about Pam's family loyalty that Tara did. Despite the legal implications of the discovery, Piper couldn't help but feel heartened to know Pam really had been willing to do whatever necessary to save their sister.

The report repeated much of what they'd read in the news articles, just with a bit more detail. Piper scanned through it. There was only detail she was interested in. The report named all the agents who'd been involved in the raid. The name of the agent who'd shot Castillo was—

"Jay Larson," Piper read aloud. The name sounded familiar.

"That's the FBI agent I told you about," Cade said. "The one who was here yesterday looking for you."

So that was it. It was all coming together. "That's not a coincidence."

"No," Cade said grimly. "For him to be here, for him to be looking for you, he has to know Castillo wants the information and that he kidnapped Tara to force Pam to provide it. He must have been the man who shot at us."

"All right, so Larson is the man who killed Castillo's son," Piper said. "Pam must have told him about the kidnapping before she knew it was him. He knew that his was the name Castillo wanted, and he must have been worried she would turn it over in exchange for Tara."

"I wonder if there's more to the story of Ricardo Castillo's death," Cade noted. "The report seems to have concluded it was justified, but it says that Larson was the only one who was with Castillo when he died. Larson says the man pulled a gun, but he's the only one alive to vouch for that. Anyone who would do what he's done the past several days just to keep his name buried isn't someone whose word I'm inclined to take."

"Me, either," she agreed. "If there is more to the story, it would possibly give him additional reasons not to want Castillo to find out about him."

"So now we likely know who was behind the kidnapping, who was responsible for Pam's accident and the attack on you, and why. What do we do about it?"

Piper shook her head, already mulling the question in her mind and not liking where her thoughts were taking her. "We can't go to the authorities with this. We don't have any proof that Larson or Castillo did anything. And even if we did have anything against Castillo, he's probably in Mexico, far out of the reach of any U.S authorities. There's no reason for him to be here. He can pay people to take care of his dirty work while he's safely out of reach."

"And if there is more to the story of Ricardo Castillo's death, you probably can't count on anyone in the FBI for help anyway. Others in the Dallas office might have been involved in any cover-up."

"So we need two things. Proof—and Castillo here in the U.S.," Piper said slowly.

"Pretty tall order," Cade said with a snort of frustration.

Indeed, Piper thought, turning the question over in her head. They needed to stop both Castillo and Larson from coming after them. It seemed like the only way to get them was to obtain those things. But how?

An idea slowly came together in her mind, a way to solve their dilemma. Her heart pounded faster as she began to think it through. It was risky and dangerous and might not even work. But if it did, it would solve everything.

If it didn't—

Well, she couldn't afford to think about that.

Remembering what Cade thought of her last desperate plan, she doubted he would like this one any better. But the more she considered it, the more certain she was that it was their best chance—perhaps their only real one—out of this.

Piper sat up in her seat and met his eyes. "Well, if we need both proof and Castillo, then let's get them. Do you have a recorder of some kind?"

He frowned. "Not really. I think there's one on my cell phone though. Why?"

"The only proof I think we can get is to have them admit what they did."

"That would work, but how are you going to get them to do that?"

"I'll get recordings of them admitting it without their knowledge. You said Larson gave you his card?" He nodded. "I'll call Larson and demand a meeting, saying I know he was the agent who killed Ricardo Castillo and threatening to give it to Esteban Castillo if he doesn't give me money…let's say, for Pam's care."

"You think he would buy that?"

"He's trying to find me. He must believe Pam got his name to me somehow, otherwise he never would have bothered trying to stop me from meeting the kidnappers. And even if he doesn't, he'll still want to show up, because he's going to try to kill me. He can't let me possess the information and risk me sharing it with anyone else, whether or not I continue to blackmail him with it."

His frown deepening, he shook his head. "Why do all your plans involve putting your life in danger?"

"My life is already in danger. He's coming after me either way, after all of us. At least this way we might be able to get out of it. Not to mention if I get in contact with him now, it should also keep his focus on me for the immediate future instead of Pam. Once he comes,

I'll get him to hopefully say enough to incriminate himself, then before he can leave either you or Matt can call the police to have them arrest him. Same with Castillo."

"How do you expect to get Castillo here?" Cade asked.

"The only thing I think would work is if I say I have the information he wants and refuse to give it to anyone but him."

"He'll just threaten to kill Pam again unless you tell him."

"I'll tell him that if he kills her he definitely won't get the information. I'm offering him the name of the man who killed his son. He's gone to all this trouble. He's not going to be able to resist it."

"You really think he'll come himself?"

"I'm sure of it. I have the name of the person who killed his son. His people already screwed up when they didn't know it was me, not Pam, who he was talking to and when they let us take Tara back. He's not going to risk them screwing this up, too."

"He'll have to suspect it's some kind of trap. Even if he didn't, he'd probably show up with an army of men that would outnumber us and make it impossible for us to get away."

"So the meeting will have to take place somewhere he can't bring a bunch of men with him without drawing too much attention. It'll have to be in public. Probably somewhere indoors, not out in the open."

"Do you really think he'll come himself and meet you in public?"

"He will. He won't be able to help himself. Because this time I really do have what he wants." She considered the possibilities. "How far is the nearest town from here?"

"About ten miles."

"Is there any place you think could work for a meeting? Maybe a restaurant or some kind of public building?"

"Dunhill's not a very big town. There's not much to it. Millie's Café is the only restaurant. It's not too big, and Castillo wouldn't be able to bring a bunch of people in there without it looking suspicious."

"Perfect. You can be there, and Matt too if he's willing to back me up."

His reaction told her that went without saying. "What makes you so sure Castillo will come?"

"Because he wants to kill me, too."

His heavy frown said what he thought of that answer. "I really don't like this."

She gave him a small smile. "I didn't think you would. But it's the only way."

She waited for him to argue and offer an alternate plan. He didn't, his expression tense with frustration, and she knew he hadn't come up with one. Because there wasn't one. The more they'd gone over the idea, the more she'd been forced to answer his challenges, the more her certainty had grown that this could work.

Once again, she was going to have to rely on one desperate plan to try to make everything all right.

And once again, failure was not an option.

Chapter Fourteen

"There has to be another way," Tara said. The young woman's chin jutted in a way Cade already recognized from her sister. It appeared to be a common trait among the Lowry women, along with being stubborn and argumentative.

"There isn't," Piper insisted from the other side of the dining room table where they'd gathered to go over her plan. "If there was, I would be doing it, believe me. So unless you have any better ideas, this is the plan."

Tara's jaw merely tightened further, as though she wanted to argue, yet couldn't, but wasn't about to admit it. They'd been going over the details for the past thirty minutes, and Piper had explained everything thoroughly. Cade had spent every one of those minutes, and every one since she'd first explained her plan to him, trying to find alternatives—no matter how remote the possibility—that could work better than what she'd come up with. He still hadn't come up with anything. They all understood the risks, the reasons and the possible rewards. That didn't make it any easier to accept, as Tara's reaction certainly proved.

For a moment, Cade forgot the seriousness of the subject at hand as his mouth curved slightly in a wry grin. He already liked the young woman. They'd met officially at lunch, and while she'd still been a little wary, she'd been a completely different person than the understandably shell-shocked young woman he'd met last night. She was just so alive, with bright eyes and a smile that was shy and sweet.

It couldn't be more obvious she and Piper were sisters. Tara looked like a younger version of Piper, with her dark hair and uncannily similar features. At the same time, she was very much a young woman, barely more than a girl. She was young and unformed, lacking the strength and maturity that Piper possessed, still an earlier version merely hinting at the person she would one day become.

She nearly hadn't had the chance, and still might not, Cade acknowledged, anger stirring in his gut. Just the thought of this girl in the hands of those men who'd arrived last night was enough to fill him with fresh rage and a wish that he'd gotten off a few shots. It hadn't taken him long to see the special bond the two women shared, and while he still might not think anything was worth Piper sacrificing her life, he could understand better than ever why she'd been willing to do so.

It was also clear the young woman wasn't intimidated by her sister and was perfectly willing to go toe-to-toe with her, as she glared at Piper. "I don't want you risking your life for me again," she said. "I love you, and I appreciate everything you've always been willing to do for me. But you don't have to take this stupid, dangerous risk for me."

"This isn't just about you," Piper said. "It's about me, too. These people are coming after me—after all of us—and this may be our only way of stopping them. Which is exactly what we're going to do. We're going to put an end to this permanently, and then we'll be safe."

Cade watched her speak, her words full of confidence, her lovely face firm with determination. She really was amazing. Listening to her, seeing her speak, he wouldn't have been surprised if she was ready to go in and take on these bastards single-handedly, without a second thought, and win. She was stronger than just about anyone, man or woman, he'd ever met. Somehow it made her even more beautiful. The idea of anything happening to her—

No. He immediately recoiled at the thought. Nothing was going to happen to her. She thought her family was worth fighting for, but damn it, she was, too. She needed someone to fight for her as strongly as she was willing to fight for everyone else. She deserved that.

He glanced back at Tara to find her studying him, her eyes narrowed. Her gaze slowly slid from him to Piper and back again. The gleam he saw flashing in those brown depths sent a flicker of unease through him. Whatever the young woman was thinking, he could tell he wouldn't like it.

When she finally spoke, it was directly to him, her expression utterly serious. "If she does this, you'll watch out for her, won't you?"

"Yes," he said without the slightest hesitation. "We both will," he added, nodding toward Matt who stood a few feet away.

Tara's attention never moved to Matt, remaining solely on Cade, as though he were the only one she cared about. He didn't blink or look away, willing to give her as long as she needed to judge his sincerity. She continued to stare at him for a long moment before nodding shortly, as though to herself, almost with satisfaction.

She looked at Piper again, her features softening. "Nothing better happen to you," Tara said fiercely, her voice still cracking slightly.

Piper reached across the table and gripped her hand tightly. "It won't."

She didn't hesitate any more than he had, her voice ringing with absolute certainty, like she didn't have a doubt in the world.

Which she shouldn't, he thought, even if she didn't know why. Because nothing was going to happen to her. He'd said the words in his head at the exact same time she had, vowing it to himself as much as to her. Nothing was going to happen to her. He wasn't going to let it, no matter what it took. He felt the conviction deep in his bones, more than he'd ever known anything before.

The sensation that he was being watched drew his gaze back to Tara, who was eyeing him shrewdly, as though she knew exactly what he was thinking, and intended to hold him to his word.

He stared back once more, giving her a small nod. She could hold him to it as much as he would himself.

This may be a crazy plan that might not have a chance in hell of working, but no matter what else happened, nothing was going to happen to Piper.

Nothing.

THEY WASTED NO TIME putting her plan into motion.

Handing Piper the business card Larson had left with him, Cade gave her his cell phone and quickly taught her how to use the voice recorder.

She dialed the number on the cell phone the kidnapper had provided, then set the phone on speaker. As soon as it began to ring, she activated the recorder on Cade's phone, placing it close enough to hers that it should pick up everything.

The line rang three times before someone answered. "Larson."

So this was what he sounded like. Piper felt a surge of anger at him, another faceless man on the phone who'd caused them so much trouble. She managed to keep her voice calm. "Agent Larson, this is Piper Lowry. I heard you're looking for me."

A long silence echoed across the line. "Yes, Ms. Lowry. That's correct."

"Well, here I am."

"So you are. I have to admit, I'm surprised that you're contacting me."

"Because you think I've been trying to deliver classified information to criminals? We both know that isn't true."

"Is that why you're calling me, Ms. Lowry? To proclaim your innocence?"

"No need. Like I said, we both already know I'm innocent. No, I'm calling to let you know about a few things I know now. I know it was you who drove my sister off the road and is responsible for her being in a coma. I know you were the agent who killed Ricardo Castillo, and mostly likely you were trying to stop Pam from providing that information to Esteban Castillo, since he's clearly trying to avenge his son's death and would have you killed."

"This is all very interesting, Ms. Lowry," he said slowly, a disinterested note in his voice. "Why are you telling me this?"

"Because I want money. The doctors are saying my sister may not awaken for many years. The medical bills are easily going to be more than I can afford and her insurance will cover. I'm looking for enough money to cover those bills. Considering that you're the person responsible for putting her in the hospital, it only makes sense that you should have to pay for her care."

"Why would I pay you? Because you've made up some ridiculous story?"

"No, because I have the FBI file on Castillo's shooting, the one that explains how you were the agent who fired the fatal shot. Pam emailed it to herself—and to me."

He didn't say anything for a moment, and she knew she'd caught him off guard. "I don't believe you," he finally said.

Piper chuckled softly. "Fine. Don't believe me. Maybe I don't have the file. Even if I didn't, I could still go ahead and tell Castillo it was you. Do you really think he'd know the difference? Do you really think he'd stop to question it before going ahead and having you killed?"

The man's silence said he didn't believe it any more than she did. "So why don't you try to sell the information to Castillo? I'm sure he could pay you far more than I can."

"The man kidnapped my sister. His men terrorized her. I have no intention of giving him what he wants and letting him win."

"But you're willing to give me what I want even though you think I tried to kill your sister."

"I don't think you want to pay me. And like I said, you should have to pay for her care, since you put her in that hospital bed."

Another silence. She could practically hear

the man grinding his teeth in anger. "How much?"

"Five hundred thousand dollars."

"I can't raise that much anytime soon."

"All right, let's make it two-hundred-and-fifty thousand. That should be enough. For now." She dragged out the final words, letting them hang in the air.

"By when?"

"Tomorrow morning. I'll be in touch." She hung up quickly before he could respond and turned off the recorder.

"He's a cool one," Cade noted gravely.

"That's for sure," Piper agreed. She would have been surprised if he hadn't been given all the things they believed him capable of.

"Scary cool," Tara said. "Like somebody you shouldn't be messing around with."

"Unfortunately, I don't have a choice," Piper said. "Because he fully intends to mess with us—and has," she amended. "But he's not going to get away with it any more."

No one responded. Whether it was because they were doubtful or deciding to take her word for it, Piper wasn't sure. She didn't bother looking up to see their faces, not really wanting to know.

Instead, she glanced down at the phone. Step

One was complete. Now on to step two. Larson was bad enough, but Castillo was far worse, something she figured she was better off not mentioning.

"Now I just need the kidnapper to get in touch."

THE CELL PHONE RANG at 5:00 p.m.

Piper had kept it within arm's reach all afternoon. Everyone in the kitchen—Piper, Cade, Matt, Tara—froze, their attention immediately going to the device buzzing on the tabletop. The four people in this room knew what it would mean when it rang. And now it finally had.

Piper was ready. Calming her nerves, she turned on the recorder, picked up the phone and took the call. "Piper Lowry."

As with Jay Larson, there was an initial beat of silence. This time she suspected Castillo was caught off guard by the confidence in her voice. "So it is," he said after a few seconds. "I thought I would check on your progress."

"It's done. I have the names of the agents involved in the raid—and the name of the agent who pulled the trigger on the bullet that killed Ricardo Castillo."

She heard a quick intake of breath. "Tell me," he nearly hissed.

"No. I'll give you the file, but only in person."

"You are in no position to make demands, Miss Lowry. Not if you care about your sister's life."

"I can make demands as long as I have what you want. If anything happens to my sister, you won't get what you want. It's as simple as that."

Another silence, this one saying he knew he'd been bested and sure as hell didn't like it. "When?" he demanded.

"Tomorrow morning. Call me at 9:00 a.m. and I'll tell you where. Oh, and Mr. Castillo? Don't just send one of your underlings. You really are going to want to be here for this, so you should start traveling to the U.S. if you're not here already. The agent who killed your son will be at the meeting, too."

As soon as she'd uttered the final words, she quickly disconnected the call and started to lower the phone. Only then did she realize her hand was shaking.

Tara was the first one to speak and break the silence that fell over the room. "You were amazing," she breathed, her eyes shining with admiration. "I've never seen you like that."

"I have," Cade said softly.

She met his eyes, the look in them making her heart twist in her chest. There was admiration there, too, and respect, but also a concern that seemed all too intimate.

"What happens now?" Tara asked, drawing Piper's attention away from Cade.

"Now we wait until morning."

She knew it would get here before they knew it, but as she glanced at the clock, it seemed impossibly far away. Larson and Castillo weren't the only ones being kept waiting. Everyone in this room had a long night ahead of them of waiting, and wondering what would happen tomorrow.

Matt pushed away from the counter. "I should get some work done."

"I should, too," Cade said, climbing to his feet. He looked down at Piper. "You two going to be okay in here?"

"Of course," Piper said. "We'll be fine."

With a nod, Cade reached for his Stetson, placing it on his head.

Piper watched him go, remembering that close moment in the office.

When he was gone, she finally glanced back at Tara to find her sister studying her, a small smile playing against her lips.

"What?" Piper asked uneasily.

"You like him."

Piper blinked at her, suddenly uncomfortable.

"Of course I like him. He's done so much to help us."

Tara tilted her head and gave her a pointed look. "That's not what I mean, and you know it. The way you were looking at him, you like him in a way that has nothing to do with gratitude."

"You're imagining things. I barely know the man. I met him yesterday."

"That's more than enough time to know if you're attracted to somebody. Or even more than that."

As Piper knew all too well. Still she shook her head. "You're imagining things."

"No, I'm not," Tara said firmly. "I've never seen you look at anyone that way." She grinned. "Took long enough."

"Even if you're right, this isn't the time. I have more important things to think about. We're playing with fire here. There's no telling how tomorrow is going to go."

Tara sobered. "You're right," she agreed softly. "This might not work. I don't want to think about it, but we both know something could go horribly wrong. But doesn't that just mean this *is* the time? Because if not now, when?"

She didn't wait for an answer, pushing away

from the table and, with one last sympathetic but pointed look, headed out of the room.

Piper remained seated at the table for a long while after she left, Tara's words echoing in her ears, the memory of that moment with Cade playing over and over in her mind.

It was a good thing Tara hadn't waited for Piper to reply to her question.

Because Piper, who'd always been there to answer Tara's questions over the years, had no answer for that one.

Chapter Fifteen

A little after one in the morning, Cade made a check of the perimeter of the house, circling the building and looking for any signs the area had been breached or any intruders were nearby. It wasn't the house he was most concerned about, though, as he stopped every few yards and gazed into the night.

The vast area of his spread had never felt anything but satisfying to him. Usually when he looked out at the land beyond the house and knew that everything as far as the eye could see was his, he was filled with a sense of pride and contentment. But on this night, as he peered into the darkness surrounding the house, he simply felt uneasy, tension knotting in his gut. The house was secure enough. The real trouble lay in whether they would realize danger was approaching before it was too late. There was no telling what could be out there in the dark.

He didn't know if anyone would try to make

a move tonight. Somehow he doubted it, though he had to hope it wasn't a case of wishful thinking on his part. In all likelihood, Larson wouldn't make a move and run the risk that Piper had sent the information to someone else in the event that something happened to her. Castillo might be more willing to get to her now that he believed she had what he wanted, especially if he wanted to show her that he wasn't going to let her dictate the terms. But if his men tried to take her and something went wrong, she could end up hurt or killed and unable to give him what he wanted. It would be easier to wait for the meeting tomorrow.

No, as far as Cade could work out, nothing should happen tonight, but he wasn't about to be unprepared.

Finally as satisfied as he could be that he didn't detect any signs of trouble, he opened the back door and stepped into the darkened kitchen. He made no move to turn on the light. It was probably better to keep it off so no one would be able to spot his location, just in case the house was being watched.

A sudden flash of motion in the corner of his vision had him jerking up his gun and slapping the light switch on the wall in two heartbeats.

Piper stood against the kitchen counter, eyes

wide, the handle of a frying pan clutched in her hands as she held the object over her shoulder, as though ready to defend herself with it.

It wouldn't have done her much good against a bullet.

He sucked in a breath, all too aware of how close a call that had been.

He could have shot her.

Trying to calm the adrenaline surging through his veins, Cade eased his finger off the trigger and slowly lowered the gun. When she was no longer in its sights, Piper took a shuddery breath of her own. "You scared me," she whispered.

"Same to you." He grimaced. "What are you doing up?"

"I couldn't sleep. Thought I might get a snack."

"In the dark?"

"I didn't think I should turn on the light in case anyone was watching the house and could see through the window."

Exactly what he'd thought, he acknowledged. He flipped the lights off, plunging the room back into darkness, with only the moonlight streaming through the windows offering any illumination. Now that he knew where she was, he could discern her outline, though she remained a vague, shadowy presence. He automatically moved closer to see her better.

"You hungry?" he asked.

"Not really," she admitted. "It was more about finding something to do instead of pacing in my room."

"Nervous about tomorrow?"

"Yes. Shouldn't I be?"

Basic logic said she should be. And yet, he hated the idea of her being nervous or scared at all. He wished he could make it better, could make it possible for her to relax, even smile.

She shot him a sardonic look and he realized he hadn't responded. "Thank you for not lying to me. I appreciate that."

"You're no fool. You know the risks you're taking. It was your plan."

"You're right. I was standing here thinking about those risks and everything that could go wrong."

"Don't," he said. "You'll just drive yourself crazy that way. I know it's hard, but try to think of something enjoyable to take your mind off it, if you can."

"That's what I was trying to do," she said, nodding toward the window over the sink. "I noticed the view from the window and couldn't help admiring it. It's beautiful here."

He didn't argue with her there. He couldn't imagine ever wanting to live anywhere else. "Have you been to New Mexico before?"

"No, I'd never been west of Pennsylvania before this trip."

"Ever wanted to travel?"

"Sure. Never had the chance."

He frowned. "Tara's been in college, what—one, two years now? You didn't have time after she left home?"

"I guess so. I just haven't really thought about it."

"You said you stayed home and got into accounting to take care of your mother and sister. Your mother's dead, your sister's gone. You can do whatever you want. What do you want to do?"

She chuckled lightly. "I can't quite do whatever I want. I still have Tara's education to pay for."

"But you can do a hell of a lot more than I bet you've done. What do you want to do?" he repeated.

She was quiet for a long time before finally shrugging halfheartedly. "I don't know," she admitted softly. "I haven't thought about that yet. If everything works out tomorrow, hopefully I'll have a chance to."

"Everything's going to work out tomorrow," he said firmly, refusing to believe otherwise.

Piper looked at him. "You're always so certain about everything. Listening to you, I'd think you didn't have a doubt in the world about what's going to happen."

He didn't—not any that he was willing to let her see anyway. "Good," he said gruffly. "Then keep listening until you believe it, too."

A small smile played against her lips. Of amusement? To humor him? He didn't know. He wasn't sure he cared. Because the smile wasn't much of one, but it was what he'd wanted, to see her smile, and a curious lightness filled his chest at the sight of it and the knowledge that he'd been the one to inspire it.

She turned her head again to peer out the window. He found himself staring at her profile, every flawless feature captured in silvery moonlight.

"Your ranch really is beautiful," she said, a wistful note in her voice.

"I wish you'd gotten to see it under different circumstances."

"Me, too. But at least I'm getting to see it now."

The words affected him more than they should. He'd heard this before. But somehow

Piper seemed so much more genuine when she said it than Caitlin ever had. Caitlin, who'd said she wanted this life, wanted him. Forever.

And she'd been from the area, knew what ranching life was about. A woman like Piper, who'd always lived in a city, had no idea what it was like. She could probably never be happy with a life here. She'd probably hate it more than Caitlin had in the end.

He nearly shook his head. What did it even matter?

He glanced down at her, only then realizing just how close he'd moved toward her. They were only a few inches apart. He wouldn't even have to raise his arm halfway to touch her. His fingers flexed involuntarily, ready to do just that.

She suddenly turned to face him, her intake of breath audible, her mouth opening as if she was on the verge of saying something.

Whatever it might have been, the words never came. He watched her register how close he was, her eyes widening, her lips closing slightly but not altogether. He recognized that he should probably step back and give her some space. Every instinct in his body fought against it, wanting only to get closer to her, to feel her body pressed against his. Using every last bit of strength in his body, he held himself where he was. He watched her expression closely for any indication she was uncomfortable, ready to force his body to step back if he saw anything.

He found none. She simply looked up at him, her eyes dark and unreadable.

He had to touch her. The compulsion was so strong and instinctive he couldn't begin to deny it.

Without even thinking about it, he lifted his hand and raised it to her face, cupping her cheek in his palm, his fingers molding to the curve of her face. A shudder quaked through him from head to toe at the contact. He took in the sight of his big, rough hand on her cheek almost with a sense of wonderment. This couldn't be real, that he was touching something, someone, so beautiful, so soft.

She didn't object, didn't try to push him away. Instead she turned her face into his palm, increasing the contact. Her eyes drifted shut, a shuddery breath emerging from her parted lips. His heart kicked up another notch, pounding against the wall of his chest, as he absorbed the sensation of her soft skin. Her lips looked even softer. They trembled slightly with each breath. He couldn't tear his eyes away. His thumb was so close, it would take nothing to reach over and stroke it over her mouth, to see if it felt as soft as it looked. It wouldn't take much more to lean forward and touch his mouth to hers, to discover if they felt as soft against his own, to taste them, to taste her.

Before he could even decide if he wanted to do such a foolish thing, she placed a staying hand against his chest. "I can't do this," she whispered. "Tara's down the hall."

The feeling of her soft, small hand against his chest nearly overwhelmed the groan that rose in his throat at her words. He could handle her putting the brakes on something that was probably a very bad idea for both of them, but not her hiding behind her sister again.

"You're always thinking about Tara," he said gently. It wasn't an accusation but an observation, and he couldn't quite keep the admiration out of his tone. He did admire her devotion to her family, but even so… "When are you going to start thinking about what you want?"

She stared up at him, her eyes stroking over his face, unblinking. He felt the heat of her gaze pouring into him like the flame from a blowtorch, searing through him.

Her attention arrived at his mouth and stayed there. She swallowed, her own mouth automatically closing for a brief moment and drawing his attention again. So very close. It would take a heartbeat—maybe even less—to lower his head, to capture her lips with his.

It would be a mistake. He knew better than to get any more involved than they already were.

He knew it. He was just having a hard time believing that kissing her would be a mistake.

A second later, she pushed up on her toes and pressed her mouth to his.

IN THE INSTANT BEFORE their lips met, Piper knew she'd found the answer to the question Cade had posed.

What do you want to do?

This.

She couldn't remember the last time she'd wanted anything—certainly not anyone—as much as she wanted this, to experience what his mouth tasted like, felt like. To feel the sensation of his body pressed against hers once more.

And then she got what she wanted, as their lips came together. His were soft yet firm as they brushed against hers, a caress she felt down to her toes. The initial contact gradually gave way to another, their mouths parting all too soon then finding each other again. He kissed her slowly, with a tenderness that stirred an ache deep in her chest. His tongue slipped forward into her mouth, unerringly finding hers, sliding against it and teasing it to respond. She did, wanting more of that delicious friction, matching him stroke for stroke as their tongues tangled in a delicate dance. Their lips met, moved together in a perfect rhythm. He took his time, and she did, too, wanting every caress of his mouth over hers, every slide of their tongues against each other, to last as long as possible.

His arms went around her, pulling her closer. She found her arms pressed against his chest and smoothed her hands down the front of his shirt. Beneath her fingers and palms she felt the hard ridges of his chest, the broad width of his shoulders. They felt as good beneath her hands as they had against her back. If only he wasn't wearing the shirt, she thought with a pang of frustration. She wanted to feel more of him, more of his skin. Even as she thought it, her hands slid higher. She wound her arms around his neck, her fingers sliding into his thick hair. It was so soft to the touch, his skin hot beneath it.

He leaned forward, and the hard edge of something pushed into her lower back, sending a jolt of pain through her. It took her a second to recognize what it was.

The edge of the kitchen counter.

They were in the kitchen.

She fought every instinct and desire in her body to tear her mouth from his, though she didn't release his face. He stared down at her, his eyes whirling with desire and confusion. She understood exactly what he was feeling. No part of her wanted to stop either. But...

"We shouldn't do this here," she whispered. "Anyone could..."

She watched comprehension dawn on his face, quickly morphing into resolve. "We should go to a bedroom."

A thrill raced through her. "Yes," she whispered.

For a split second, his face creased in a grin so big and dazzling her heart nearly stopped dead in her chest at the sight of it. She'd never seen him smile like that. He was handsome enough with his normal, stoic expression, but it was nothing compared to his smile.

Then he was stepping back and grabbing her hand. He didn't have to pull her with him. She sprang into motion right when he did. They hurried out of the kitchen and into the hall.

They made their way down the back hallway as quietly as possible, moving in unison on the balls of their feet. Her room was the second door to the left—next to Tara's, she registered.

Before she could even slow to consider whether they should go there, he was moving to a room to the right and opening the door.

His, she registered as she took in the room in a glance, getting a quick impression of male furnishings. She barely noticed most of the room, her eyes going to the bed in the middle. It was big and wide. He hadn't made it that day, the covers already thrown back as though waiting to be climbed into.

"Are you sure about this?" he asked behind her with a tenderness that nearly made her heart melt completely in her chest, until there was nothing in her body but pure, molten heat.

She looked back to find he'd closed the door and was standing in front of it, the same question in his eyes.

She answered by reaching for the buttons on his shirt and starting to release them. With each successive one, she picked up speed, her fingers seeming clumsier and clumsier the closer she came to baring him to her and getting what she wanted. Finally the shirt was completely open, revealing a white T-shirt underneath. He wasted no time shrugging out of the outer shirt. By the time he reached down for the bottom of the T-shirt, her hands were already there, pushing it upward, her knuckles grazing against the hard ridges on his firm, flat belly.

With a low growl, he yanked it completely over his head, sending it flying across the room. It was little more than a blur at the edge of her vision. She didn't bother to watch it go, unable to tear her gaze away from what she'd revealed.

He was magnificent, even more than she'd known he would be. She'd felt that body pressed up against her back when they were on his horse, felt it beneath her fingers in the kitchen. She knew those muscles, remembered how they felt, but it was something else altogether to see how they looked. His shoulders were wide and broad, his arms big and muscled. Dark hair lightly dusted his pecs and belly, a line of it trailing into the low-hanging waistband of his jeans. She followed it with her eyes, then lower past his belt buckle, until she found herself staring at the heavy bulge jutting against the fly of his jeans.

Her mouth went dry at the sight of it. Unable to resist, she reached down and cupped her hand there, feeling the hard ridge pressing insistently under the worn denim. Her hand couldn't contain it all, the ridge longer than the length from the tip of her fingers to the heel of her palm.

He groaned, the sound so choked in his throat it was barely audible. She didn't need to hear the reaction. She felt it, as he suddenly lunged forward and swept her clear off her feet. He carried her to the bed, gently lowering her on the mattress and sitting beside her. As he reached down for his boots, she immediately began to shrug out of her clothes, tossing aside her T-shirt, shimmying out of her jeans. The whole time she kept her eyes on him, watching the muscles of his back shift beneath the smooth skin as he tugged off his boots, first one then the other. Then, he rose again, unfastening his belt and the button on his jeans with fast, jerky motions. Shoving his thumbs into the waistband, he shoved the jeans down his hips, taking his underwear with them, leaning forward as he did so, giving her a prime view of his behind. It was as firm and muscled as the rest of him. She immediately stopped, unable to do anything but take in the sight. She could have stared all day.

Cade didn't give her a chance. As soon as he'd kicked out of the jeans, he straightened and turned to face her.

He stood before her, completely nude, the sight taking her breath away. And she'd thought his mere chest had been magnificent, or that he'd looked good from the rear. It couldn't com-

pare to the full view, his body hard and firm
from head to toe, his erection jutting straight
out, as big and thick as the rest of him.

Then he was moving forward, climbing onto
the bed beside her. She scooted backward on
the mattress so they could both stretch out, and
realized she hadn't removed her panties. Before
she could move to do so, his hands were already
there, his fingers slipping into the waistband
and gently drawing it away from her skin. She
raised her hips and let him pull them down her
thighs. His fingertips grazed her skin, the touch
so light she barely felt it, but enough to stir the
aching need to have him touch her.

When she was finally as bare as he was,
he reached for her. An instant later, his large,
warm hands were finally on her, skimming over
her side, finding her breasts. His fingers and
palms were big and slightly rough, the skin of
a man who worked with his hands. She'd never
quite felt anything like it, the sensation of them
against her soft skin creating a delicious friction wherever they made contact. She basked
in the feeling of it, even as she reached out to
touch him, threading her fingers through his
chest hair, finally feeling his amazing body
beneath her hands. He caught her mouth once
more, kissing her deeply as they explored each

other's bodies. It was all more than she could begin to process, the feeling of his mouth, of his hands on her, of hers on him, surrounding her in exquisite sensation.

Then one of his hands smoothed its way down her belly until his fingertips found her damp folds. He teased her for just the slightest of moments, a moment that still felt like an eternity, rubbing her lightly with the tip of one finger before sliding it inside her. A thrill shot through her at the invasion as he gently explored, testing her readiness, first with one finger, then two. She tightened her muscles around him, reveling in the sensation, knowing it was a mere taste of so much more to come.

His fingers suddenly pulled away. She opened her mouth to object, a whimper nearly bursting from her throat. He rolled away, and she watched him lean forward, unable to keep her eyes from stroking over the length of his body, the muscular torso, the hard thighs and long legs. He reached into the bedside table and pulled out a foil packet. Tearing it open, he covered himself within seconds, then returned to her, stretching out beside her.

He'd barely done so when he moved over her, rolling her onto her back, bracing himself above her on one arm, nudging her legs apart with his knee and positioning himself between them. It felt as though he was completely surrounding her on all sides, the sensation overwhelming in a wonderful way. He was everywhere, and yet somehow she didn't have enough of him. She wanted more.

Then she felt the tip of his erection between her thighs, nudging her, seeking entrance. Anticipation spiked in her chest. She peered up into his eyes as he looked back at her, his eyes smoky with desire and an unspoken question she had no trouble understanding. He wanted to know if she was ready. She let her smile answer for her.

The corner of his mouth curved in a slow, achingly sexy grin and he pushed inside her, filling her with one long, hard, sure thrust. She immediately exhaled, the sound full of the contentment she felt welling through her. It was so good, so right. She never took her eyes from his, her smile deepening to match his, almost giddy from the rightness of this moment.

In a heartbeat, he lowered his head and claimed her mouth, even as he pulled his hips back and thrust again. Harder. Deeper. A moan burst from her throat, swallowed by his mouth on hers. He kissed her as slowly and tenderly as he had in the kitchen. When he finally pulled away, he remained close, his face inches above hers, peering into her eyes.

She reached up and wound her fingers through his hair, wanting to hold him to her, keep him as close as possible. She gazed up into his eyes with a sense of wonder, filled with a sense of connection that was stronger than anything she'd ever felt with another person, something that went far beyond the physical link between their bodies. She watched the emotions pass across his face, saw the amazement in his eyes, and knew he felt it, too, this strange, unexpected connection.

They built a rhythm together, his hips slowly retreating and pushing forward again, hers rising to meet him. The intensity built along with their speed. Piper tried to hold on as long as she could, not wanting to let go of this moment, even as she felt herself being pushed higher than she'd ever experienced before. She read in his eyes, on his face, in the tensing of his body over hers, how close he was to the edge.

Until, finally, unable to hold on any longer, they erupted together, sheer pleasure exploding through her body and filling every last bit of her. Through it all, she stared up into his eyes, helpless to do anything else but look at the tenderness in this man's gaze, even as she felt it deep in her bones.

And as she floated out of the delicious haze, she realized this wasn't what she'd wanted.

It was so much more.

More than she'd ever dreamed of for herself, more than she'd ever thought possible.

Just like the man who'd made it happen.

"TELL ME ABOUT YOUR WIFE."

Curled up beside him—her head on his chest, her arm slung across his belly—Piper felt Cade tense in response to her quietly asked question.

"Why?"

She had to admit it probably wasn't the most natural topic for pillow talk, but she also couldn't hold back her curiosity any longer. She wanted to know everything about this man, now more than ever after what they'd just shared, and this was a key piece of the puzzle she was missing.

"Because she's come up a lot in the past few days. I'd like to understand why. What was her name again?"

"Caitlin," he muttered.

Cade and Caitlin. Even their names sounded like they belonged together, she thought with a completely illogical pang of envy.

"Matt said you met because she was in trouble."

He swore under his breath. "Matt talks too much."

"So what happened?"

"She was living with a guy in town, name of Horton. He wasn't treating her right. I'd never paid much attention to her before, but one day in town I saw him shove her and start to hit her. I stepped in and made him back off. She threw her arms around me, and that was it. Seemed like we were together from then on. She didn't have anywhere else to go and Horton wasn't the kind of guy to let her go easily, so I said she could stay here. She moved right in. After a while I asked her to marry me. She said yes. We got married."

He related the story in a flat, robotic way that made it sound completely emotionless. Piper had a feeling it just showed how affected by it he still was.

"What happened?"

"She left one day, with one of the hands. Left a note saying she wasn't cut out for ranch life, needed more than this. That was it. A month later, the divorce papers came in the mail."

"Did you try to track her down?"

"No."

"Why not?"

"Why bother? I didn't want to make her stay if she didn't want to be here. I knew she wasn't happy here toward the end. It was too isolated, too boring. The guy she left with was a short-timer with dreams of joining the rodeo circuit. I'm sure the life he had to offer her seemed a lot more exciting than life here."

"But didn't you love her?"

He was quiet for a long moment. "Yeah," he admitted softly. "I did. Which makes me a fool, because I'm pretty sure she didn't love me, not really. She probably was just grateful to me for saving her. Guess I can understand that. Somebody comes along when you really need them and helps you out, it's probably easy to confuse gratitude for something else."

Something about the way he said it, so heavy with significance, gave her pause, and she froze, an uneasy feeling rising from the pit of her stomach.

"Is that why you think I'm here right now?"

He didn't say anything for a long moment, the silence answer enough. "You tell me."

Her heart sinking, she slowly pulled away from him, gathering the sheet around herself. His arm immediately slackened, making no effort to hold her close. "If you don't know, then I probably shouldn't be here at all."

She heard him draw in a breath, as though to say something. She didn't wait for it, sitting upright and swinging her legs over the side of the bed.

It was a good thing she hadn't waited. Whatever he might have been about to say, nothing came out.

Pushing off the bed, she tied the sheet around her, then bent down and quickly gathered up her clothes. Pulling them tightly to her like a lifeline, she rose and moved toward the door.

She felt his eyes on her the whole way there, his gaze boring into her back. With each step that took her closer to the door, she waited for him to call after her, to say something, anything at all.

He didn't. The silence stretched on, carrying her out of the room.

Her room was almost exactly across the hall. As soon the door was safely shut behind her, she sagged against it, releasing a breath she hadn't known she was holding.

What a humiliating end to what had been one of the best experiences of her life. Hard to believe that only a few minutes ago, she'd been more content, more relaxed, just plain happier than she'd been in a long time.

It hurt to think that he could believe that of her, that he suspected she was no different than this woman who'd hurt him so badly. It probably shouldn't. He had no way of knowing her motives anymore than she did his.

Yes, she liked him more than was logical, was more attracted to him than any man she'd ever remember, was far too attached to him already. But she didn't know him, not really. Didn't know what he was thinking, didn't know the inner workings of his heart. She wasn't sure anyone could possibly know that of another person, but certainly not after only a couple days.

But, oh, how she wished she did. Wished she could get to know him more. Wished there could be so much more between them than there ever could.

Except that she'd already gotten what she'd thought she'd wanted tonight.

She shouldn't push her luck by wanting anything more.

CADE WATCHED HER GO, her name on the tip of his tongue, pressing against his lips, just waiting to come out.

His mouth remained stubbornly closed. He

couldn't bring himself to do it, couldn't make himself call after her, some deeply ingrained self-preservation instinct holding him back.

And then she was gone.

He sighed, his shoulders slumping. He should have told her no, he knew that wasn't why this had happened between them. That he knew she wasn't like that. That she was nothing like Caitlin.

Except in one very big way.

Her time here was just temporary. She was stronger, smarter, more loyal, more beautiful, more *everything* than Caitlin had ever been. He'd known her for such a short amount of time, but he could see that already. She was like no other woman he'd ever met. And yet, when it came down to it, she was just another woman who was going to leave anyway. At least this time he knew it from the start. She had another life on the other side of the country, would never have crossed paths with him if it wasn't for the terrible circumstances she'd found herself in. As soon as those circumstances were resolved, she would have no reason to be here anymore.

Deep down he'd recognized that, and had known it was best for both of them if he kept his mouth shut.

He placed his hand on the spot on the mattress where she'd just been lying. It was still warm from the heat of her body. He pressed down, as though trying to draw that heat into him, trying to hold on to it, to her, as long as he could.

All too soon the warmth was gone, leaving no trace that she'd been there at all.

The same way she would soon be, and he'd be a lot better off remembering that.

Chapter Sixteen

As dawn broke over the distant horizon, Castillo stood at the bedroom window as he had so often over the past few days. He watched the skyline suddenly blaze with light, the golden glow stretching all the way across the desert to reach him. He felt the warmth of it on his face like a caress, and briefly closed his eyes, tilting his head back to let the feeling sink in.

It was going to be a beautiful day.

He hadn't slept, unable to do anything but think, preparing himself for what lay ahead.

In a few short hours he would call the Lowry woman—*Piper* Lowry, he thought with a twinge of annoyance. She would name the meeting place and he would go.

And then…

A grim smile touched his lips.

Ah, yes. And then…

It could be a trap of some sort. He knew this. Just as he knew that as long as there was any chance he would learn the name of his son's murderer—let alone see the bastard's face—he had to go.

The Lowry woman could be lying, of course. He knew that, too. But he'd spoken to her enough over the past several days to be able to read her voice, and he didn't believe she was lying. She knew who had killed Ricardo. He could feel it.

Diaz had expressed his doubts—carefully, of course, to commit no offense. Castillo had confirmed that he intended to do this. His men would scope out the location as much as possible once the Lowry woman named it. It would be somewhere public, no doubt, somewhere it would look suspicious if he arrived with all his men. They would be nearby, of course, but wherever it was, he would have to go alone.

As he'd always intended to do all along.

Yes, he knew many things, which was why he felt no doubt nor concern about what lay in store for him on this day.

Instead, for the first time in nearly a year he felt at peace.

For his son—for justice—he knew exactly what he must do.

AFTER A NEARLY SLEEPLESS night, Piper was up by seven. Last night she'd wanted something to distract her from her nervousness about the coming day. She'd certainly found that. She hadn't thought about what was going to happen this morning at all for the rest of the night.

And then it was time.

She had to focus. Setting everything else aside, she turned her attention to what lay in store for the next few hours.

The plan was for Tara to stay behind at the house where she should be safe. Piper didn't want her anywhere near town in the middle of things, where she'd be a distraction for her and a possible target for Larson, Castillo or both. None of them would be able to keep her safe in town, but with everyone's attention soon to be focused there, Tara should be fine in the house. Just to be sure of that, Cade showed her where the storm cellar was, where she could lock herself inside, and left her with a rifle. She'd never used one, but thankfully she had used a firearm before so she wasn't completely unfamiliar with the concept. Cade gave her a few quick instructions, and though Piper was sure she'd be okay, she was confident Tara would be able to handle it if she had to.

Once he'd shown her everything, he left her and Piper to say goodbye.

Standing in the doorway to the cellar steps,

Tara looked her straight in the eye. "Are you sure you want to do this?"

Piper nodded firmly. "I'm sure. It's the only way."

She read the uncertainty in Tara's gaze and forced a smile she hoped was convincing. It was more than an attempt to make Tara believe everything was going to work out. Beyond that, if this was the last time they saw each other, Piper wanted Tara to remember her smiling.

Piper couldn't tell if Tara believed her conviction before her sister drew her in for one last hug.

"Be careful," Tara whispered.

"I will," Piper promised fiercely. She had to force herself to let Tara go, and felt her sister's reluctance to do the same. Finally they pulled apart.

Piper scanned Tara's face hungrily, wanting to remember exactly how she looked in this moment. Even as she did it, she tried to tell herself it was unnecessary. They would see each other again. The plan was going to work.

It had to.

With one last look, Piper made herself turn and walk away.

They were taking two trucks into town, with Cade and Matt each driving one. The vehicles were waiting in front of the house, their engines already running and ready to go. Piper climbed into the one where Cade sat behind the wheel.

"You okay?" Cade asked after a moment when she didn't say anything.

"Fine," she said, trying not to take the question as anything more than a common courtesy.

He didn't say another word, starting the engine and shifting into gear. As the truck rumbled down the driveway, Piper glanced back at the house in the side mirror one last time, then forced herself to put Tara out of mind as much as she could and focus on what she had to do.

It was time to proceed with the plan.

As THEY LEFT THE RANCH, Piper crouched down in her seat so she wouldn't be seen, just in case either Larson or Castillo's people decided to try anything. She braced herself as the truck bumped along the driveway, waiting for the slightest sign of trouble.

The truck turned, the ride suddenly became smoother and she knew they'd hit the highway.

A few more minutes passed, her muscles straining to hold their position, her nerves fraying with each second that ticked by.

Then, finally, Cade said, "I think it's clear."

With a sigh of relief, Piper eased herself into her seat. She glanced back to see Matt's truck trailing behind. Otherwise there were no signs of any other vehicles on the road either in front of or behind them.

Neither of them spoke the rest of the drive into town. They'd barely said two words to each other that morning, and nothing was brought up about what happened between them last night. It made sense, of course. They both had more important things to think about. But Piper couldn't fool herself into thinking that was why they hadn't mentioned it.

She didn't know what to say. Whether he didn't either or simply didn't want to, she didn't know.

Dunhill turned out to be just as small as Cade said, merely a cluster of buildings along the sides of the highway. Piper spotted a gas station and a few stores, but that was about it. If she'd been driving through, she might not have considered it a town, if she even noticed before she passed straight through it.

By eight-forty they were in place. Cade parked down the street from the café. The location offered a good enough view that they would be able to see anyone entering, while also making it unlikely anyone would notice them sitting there. Matt kept going and parked on the other end of the street.

They waited in silence, still apparently having nothing to say. As the minutes ticked by, Piper could feel the tension building in the truck's silent cab. She wanted to believe it was from the anticipation of the call they were waiting for, but couldn't fool herself. There was something too personal about it. What had happened between them lay too heavily in the air, the awareness thick between them.

She tried to focus on what she had to say to the kidnapper, but she already knew it by heart, and it was nearly impossible to ignore the overwhelming presence of the man sitting beside her. It didn't matter if she turned her head and looked out the window so he was no longer even in the edge of her vision. She could still sense him there, feel him there, as if he was right in front of her.

The phone rang at exactly nine o'clock.

Showtime.

Piper immediately turned on the recorder on Cade's cell phone, then took the call on her own, activating the speaker phone. "You're right on time," she said smoothly.

"As you requested," the man said with an edge that spoke to how angry he was at having to follow her orders.

"I appreciate that. Meet me at Millie's Café

in Dunhill, New Mexico. Be there at eleven o'clock."

He fell silent. "Is this some kind of trap, Miss Lowry?"

Strangely, she didn't detect any actual concern in his tone, only mild curiosity. "What kind of trap would it be? I can't prove you did anything, can I?" *Not yet, anyway.*

"No, I suppose you can't."

"Eleven o'clock," she repeated, then hung up before he could get in another word.

Taking a breath to gird herself for round two, Piper pulled out Larson's card and began dialing.

"You're doing great," Cade said softly.

His words warmed her, but she allowed herself only a short nod of acknowledgment as she activated the speaker phone again.

The call was answered on the second ring. "Larson."

"Piper Lowry. Do you have what we discussed?"

There was a long pause before he grudgingly said, "Yes."

Why the pause? she wondered idly. Because he was angry about having to get the money, or because he was lying about getting it and he had no intention of delivering? Piper supposed it didn't really matter. All that did was that he show up.

"Then let's meet."

"Where?"

"Millie's Café in Dunhill, New Mexico. Eleven o'clock." Once again she ended the call without waiting for a response.

Shutting off the recorder, she sagged back against the seat. "And now we wait."

He nodded. They couldn't go into the diner just yet. If she loitered too long at a table, the staff might grow suspicious and want her to leave before the designated meeting time, and that couldn't happen. Their location offered a prime view of the entrance in case any of her guests arrived early. In the meantime, all they could do was wait.

She sensed before he opened his mouth that he was going to say something, her insides tensing.

"About last night…" he began.

"Don't," she said. "I know you well enough by now to know you don't like talking about emotional stuff, Cade, so I know you don't really want to talk about that now. I get the feeling you're only bringing it up because you want to make sure everything is settled between us in case something goes wrong. It won't. There *will* be time to talk about that later. If you still want to then."

"All right."

His relief was palpable, or maybe she was feeling her own. Because she didn't want to hear his apologies, didn't want to make what had happened last night sound like a mistake, which was exactly what she suspected he was going to say.

Because she didn't regret it. It had been exactly what she'd wanted, exactly what she'd needed last night. It was an experience she would remember fondly, no matter how it had ended.

It was also in the past, and at the moment all she could afford to think about was the immediate future.

LARSON WAS THE FIRST to arrive.

Piper had taken a seat at a booth against the inside wall. It offered a prime view of the entrance, and was also situated so that no one could enter from the rear and catch her off guard.

Cade and Matt had placed themselves behind her, Cade at the counter on a direct angle to her, Matt farther away. It was reassuring to know they both had her back, but Piper still felt her tension growing the longer she sat there, lingering over the cup of coffee and burger she'd ordered but couldn't begin to force down. Fortunately, the place wasn't too busy, so the waitress didn't make any effort to hurry her out. Besides the two waitresses, there were a dozen customers, including her, Cade and Matt. Less than a third of the tables were occupied. Hopefully it was a large enough crowd that Larson and Castillo wouldn't want to do anything in front of so many witnesses.

Though she'd never seen the man before, she had no trouble recognizing Larson. He matched Cade's description of him: late thirties, thinning blond hair. The dark suit and sunglasses he wore were completely out of place here. As she watched, he removed the sunglasses and scanned the room. When he spotted her, he immediately zeroed in on her and began to cross the room.

He was carrying a briefcase clutched in his right hand. Piper wondered if there was any money in it. She'd find out soon enough. She just had to hope he didn't have some kind of weapon.

She carefully turned on the recorder sitting in her lap and waited.

He stopped beside the booth opposite her and simply stood there looking down at her. He was smaller than she'd imagined, less physically intimidating, but the menace emanating from him made it impossible to forget this was a dangerous man.

"Agent Larson, I presume?" she asked when he didn't say anything.

"You know who I am," he said flatly.

Casting a glance around them, she motioned to the booth on the other side of the table. "Please have a seat. You don't want to draw any unnecessary attention, do you?"

Grimacing, he slowly slid into the booth, setting the briefcase on the seat beside him. "I could arrest you right now, force you to come with me."

"But you're not going to do that, because you don't have a warrant, do you, Agent Larson?"

"Do you think anyone here is going to ask me for one? All I'll have to do is show my ID and we'll be gone before you know it."

"You also can't be sure I don't have the information waiting to be sent to Castillo as soon as something happens to me," she retorted.

His eyes narrowed to slits. "Who else have you told what you think you have?"

She smiled. "Why would I tell you that? So you can go after them, too?"

"I don't know what you're talking about."

"Of course you do. You wouldn't be here if you hadn't hurt my sister."

"I'm here because a good friend and colleague of mine is in bad shape and I want to help her. That's what you asked me to come here for. To help Pam."

She wondered who he was trying to convince. It made no sense with how he'd started the conversation. Was he that cagey, or had he figured out she was recording this conversation and wanted him to confess?

She was going to have to try to push him harder. She nodded at the briefcase. "Is that the money?"

He glanced down at the briefcase at his side as though he'd forgotten it was there. "Yes. To help Pam."

"All two-hundred-and-fifty thousand dollars?"

There was a long pause before he admitted through gritted teeth, "Yes."

"That's a lot of help," she said wryly. "You're a really good friend, Agent Larson."

"I try to be."

The bland look on his face was starting to look too smug for her liking, and Piper felt her anger spike. This man had tried to kill Pam, had tried to kill her, had put Tara's life in jeopardy and was just sitting there, acting like they were talking about the weather. She couldn't stand it anymore.

"Why don't we quit playing games and put our cards on the table?"

"I don't know what you mean," he said.

"If Pam is such a friend, how could you try to kill her?"

He did an admirable job feigning shock. "I did no such thing. I don't even know how you can say that."

"Spare me. We both know it's true."

"I don't know any such thing."

She choked back a wave of frustration. He wasn't saying nearly enough for the recording to prove he'd done anything. Worse, he was baldly lying, that insufferable look on his face. Seething, she was tempted to throw out the trump card that had gotten him here and threaten to tell Esteban Castillo he was the agent who'd killed Ricardo if he didn't just admit it. She couldn't, of course. She couldn't threaten him into admitting it. He could claim he'd only done so to keep her from putting his life in danger, and the confession would be useless.

As she tried to figure out what to say she saw someone entering the café in the corner of her vision. She glanced over Larson's shoulder and saw a big man in his sixties standing in the doorway.

Castillo.

Even more than Larson, he looked like he didn't belong here. The suit he wore was lighter in color and less formal than Larson's, but it was still a far cry from the Western apparel everyone else in the room was wearing. His bearing was one of wealth, of someone who would never consider walking into a place like this. She immediately saw that he was drawing attention. He couldn't have been more out of place if he'd been completely nude.

And just like Larson, he spotted her and started toward her. But it wasn't her that he was focused on as he made his way to her table. His attention zeroed in on the back of the head of the man seated across from her.

This was it.

She must have looked too long and Larson must have noticed her looking over his shoulder, because he started to turn to see who she was looking at.

He didn't get a chance. Before he could even turn halfway, Castillo reached them.

The man loomed over the table. Shock flared

in both men's eyes, Larson's quickly turning to fear, Castillo's to rage.

"James Ridgeway," Castillo sneered. "I should have known."

"Ridgeway?" she said to the FBI agent. "I thought your name was Larson."

He said nothing, simply staring at Catillo.

Piper glanced between the men uneasily. "So you two already know each other?"

"He and my son were friends when they were boys," Castillo said. "Ridgeway's father was an American working in Mexico City, and James and Ricardo met in school. I always thought he was a snake, a weasel. He always let Ricardo take the blame for any trouble they got into. He and his mother left when his father died and I was glad to see him go.

"I thought you were out of my son's life for good, but you came slithering back like the snake you are, didn't you?"

"I don't know what you're talking about."

"Liar!" Castillo screamed. "I knew my son would never try to kill someone. He didn't have it in him. He was weak, but he had a good soul. If anyone tried to arrest him, he would have gone peacefully."

He jabbed a finger in Larson's face. "You

killed him deliberately, didn't you? To hide the fact that you were involved in his business with him. When your own people in the FBI got too close, you killed him!"

Larson said nothing. A vein that had started frantically working at his jaw was his only reaction.

Piper wanted to ask why he didn't even try to deny it. Did he know it was no use? Did he simply not care?

And then it didn't matter.

Castillo produced the gun from his jacket so quickly it was like he'd had it in hand the whole time. Piper barely had time to process its presence there in his grasp before he had it aimed at Larson's chest.

And pulled the trigger.

Larson jerked back in his seat, the splash of red erupting on the front of his shirt before he had time to react to the gun, before the look of surprise appeared on his face. Then he slowly lowered his head to look down at his chest before raising his eyes.

The last thing he saw was Castillo taking fresh aim at the center of his forehead.

Another explosion.

A round hole appeared in the middle of his

forehead. Piper immediately knew he was dead, his eyes glassy and unmoving, staring at nothing.

A dull roaring filled her ears. Over it, little more than a faint buzzing, came the sound of screams and raised voices.

A man said something, words she could barely make out.

Something like…"Drop it!"

The gun. He meant the gun. The gun he'd just used to shoot Larson.

Castillo didn't drop it though. He still had it gripped in his hand. She could see his finger on the trigger.

He started to turn toward her.

He didn't even make it halfway.

Another explosion rocked the room. Castillo suddenly jerked off his feet, his arms flailing wildly, the gun flying from his grasp. As he fell backward seemingly in slow motion, Piper saw the big red stain on his chest, too, one that hadn't been there before.

He landed on the linoleum floor. Piper lurched to her feet and stumbled out of the booth to look at the man.

She didn't know how long she'd been standing there when a large, firm hand settled on her shoulder. Piper was too numb with shock to flinch at the sudden, unexpected contact.

"Are you okay?" a voice asked as though from a great distance. Cade.

She found herself nodding, the sensation so disconnected it was as if it was happening to someone else. "Fine."

The hand tightened, squeezing gently, re-assuringly, the warmth managing to break through the numbness a little. "The police will be here soon."

She nodded again. They needed to talk, needed to figure out what they were going to say.

But all she could do was stare at the face of the man lying at her feet.

Castillo lay on his back, staring blindly at the ceiling.

She'd seen it with her own eyes and still couldn't believe it had really happened. They'd chosen the diner because it was in public, it was safe. No one would pull something here, among all these witnesses.

Yet Castillo had.

She wondered what he'd been thinking when he'd drawn that gun and pulled the trigger. Had he really thought he could shoot a man in broad daylight and get away with it? Or had he been so blinded by rage he hadn't thought about it?

She would never know. She supposed it didn't really matter.

He'd done it. He hadn't gotten away with it. And despite how it had ended for him, as she looked at his face, she knew he wouldn't have done anything differently.

Because he didn't look shocked or surprised or at all remorseful at the moment of his death.

No, Esteban Castillo was smiling.

Chapter Seventeen

In the end, they lied.

Piper and Cade conferred quickly before the police arrived. There didn't seem to be much point in explaining the whole story to the local authorities. Piper didn't want to be stuck there answering what would no doubt be a multitude of questions from both the local and federal authorities. She needed to get back to Dallas and check on Pam. She'd left her alone long enough as it was. And she didn't want to have to explain how she'd known Larson was the agent who killed Castillo's son, or how she'd gotten them here, didn't want to destroy Pam's career for when she did wake up.

So Cade managed to slip Larson's briefcase full of money out of the booth unnoticed, went to the bathroom and dropped it out the window to the back alley where they picked it up later. When the authorities arrived, Piper explained that she was in town visiting her friend Cade at his ranch. Larson, a colleague of her sister's, had contacted her asking to meet with her. Knowing how close they'd been, Piper had of course agreed. Cade had driven her into town, then sat separately from her so she and Larson could have some privacy. They'd been having a nice discussion when a man she'd never seen before came up and angrily confronted Larson, finally opening fire. She had no idea who he was or why he'd done such a thing.

As soon as the police learned an FBI agent had been killed, they contacted the Albuquerque field office, which immediately dispatched several agents. Piper told the same story to them. She didn't know if it was the fact that her sister was one of them, or that she was in a coma, but they didn't question her too thoroughly and seemed inclined to take her at her word.

If anyone with the FBI in Dallas wanted to speak with her, they didn't need to come here. They could find her in Dallas at her sister's bedside.

The authorities finally let them go, and they all returned to the ranch, where Tara was waiting anxiously. They'd called ahead on the way, so she knew what had happened. The trucks had barely stopped in front of the house when the front door was thrown open and Tara rushed outside.

She raced to Piper and threw her arms around her.

"It's really over?" she breathed into her neck.

"It's really over," Piper confirmed.

Tara let out a deep sigh of relief that drew a smile to Piper's lips. After everything her sister had been through, the fact that Tara was here in her arms, safe and happy, filled her with a special joy. This was what she'd been fighting for, the same way she always had, although against much higher stakes. Her family. And she'd won. They'd made it.

They finally broke apart, all too soon for Piper. "What happens now?" Tara asked.

"We go to Dallas and see Pam," Piper said. *Pam.* The reminder sent a twinge through her. Everything wasn't all right. Not yet. Pam still needed to get better. At least now she would have a chance to, without the threat of anything happening to her.

"Right." Tara nodded. "Do you think Cade would want to come?"

Piper started at the question. "Why would he?"

Tara gave her one of those inscrutable looks Piper knew meant she was thinking a lot more than she was letting on. "Do you want him to come?"

"Why would I?" she asked, even as the very idea had her heart leaping in her chest.

Which was ridiculous. They'd barely spoken on the drive back, both of them needing to process what had happened, she figured. As for anything else they may have needed to discuss... She hadn't known what to say. Apparently he hadn't either, or else he simply hadn't had anything to say at all.

Something that looked strangely like disappointment passed across Tara's face before she shrugged one shoulder. "I wouldn't know. So we're going?"

Piper nodded. "I just need to get my suitcase. Do you need anything?"

Tara shook her head. Of course she didn't. She hadn't come here with anything, so of course she didn't have anything to take. "I'll just say goodbye and thank-you to Cade and Matt."

"Good idea," Piper murmured. Quickly lowering her head, she hurried inside.

Her suitcase was packed and sitting beside the bed where she'd left it that morning. All she had to do was pick it up and go.

She walked over to it and leaned down to do

just that, only to freeze, her fingers hovering above the handle.

She wasn't ready to go.

The knowledge she'd been trying to deny burst forth, until there was no ignoring it.

She didn't want to go.

She knew she had to. She had to see to Pam. She had her job, her home, back in Boston.

She had every reason to go and no reason to stay.

Except for the simple fact that she wanted to.

She didn't want to leave this place. Didn't want to say goodbye....

But then, this wasn't her home, and she likely had no say in the matter, she reminded herself. By all indications, Cade would be happy to see her go. He'd given her no reason to think otherwise.

Shoving down the wave of emotion, she grabbed the handle on the suitcase, picked it up and strode from the room.

As soon as she stepped back onto the front porch, she spotted Tara sitting in the passenger seat of the rental car, ready to go. Matt must have pulled it out of the barn. She didn't see him. There was only one other person in sight.

Cade stood at the bottom of the steps, the Stetson pulled low over his forehead, casting a shadow that hid his eyes from her. She didn't need to see them to know he was looking at her. Heat rushed through her as she felt his steady gaze on her.

This was it.

She slowly crossed the distance between them until they were face-to-face. They stood there in silence for a long moment, just looking at each other. It was clear he wasn't sure what to say any more than she was. "Well," she finally forced herself to say. "I guess this is goodbye."

"Looks like it."

"I can't begin to thank you for everything—"

"Don't," he cut her off, his voice rough. "You don't have to say it. I know."

"I have to say it at least once," she said softly. Drawing a breath, she tried to imbue those two little words with every last bit of feeling she could. "Thank you."

"I'm glad everything worked out."

They lapsed back into an awkward silence, just looking at each other.

Ask me to stay.

As soon as the thought formed in her mind, she recognized how ridiculous it was. They'd known each other for two days. Sure, they'd been the headiest, most event-filled, intense two days of her life. It seemed as if she'd lived more

in those two days than most people did in a life-
time. Still, though, two days…

But if he asked, she would do it. She recognized that too, the idea sending a thrill
through her. She would walk away from her life
in Boston, her job, her home. She would take
that big, dumb, foolish risk, for just a chance
to see if this could be something real, if two
wildly emotional days could be the foundation
of something lasting and true.

All he had to do was ask….

The thought rose again, a plea seeming to
pour out of her very soul.

*Ask me to stay. Ask me to come back. Ask
anything at all….*

Still he said nothing, simply looking at her
steadily with those deep, unreadable blue eyes.

If only he wasn't so much the strong, silent
type.

If only she had the courage to suggest it herself.

But she couldn't. A sharp, instinctive fear
rose from the pit of her stomach at the very
idea. The image of her mother's face—that
need, that desperation—came back to her. After
watching her mother make so many mistakes
and chase after men, she couldn't do it. She

couldn't put herself out there like that. It had to come from him.

Then he nodded once, ducking his head. "Take care of yourself."

The words were gruff, almost dismissive. A token sentiment, something that made a lot more sense for people who'd known each other as long as they had. Certainly more sense than being willing to chuck it all for a virtual stranger.

A virtual stranger who she responded to more than any man she'd ever known.

A virtual stranger who didn't want her.

She forced back the disappointment that welled in her throat, thankful she hadn't said anything. The old fear had led her right, after all.

"You, too," she made herself murmur, then quickly turned away in case he looked up again and was able to see something in her expression.

Straightening her shoulders, she lifted her chin and walked toward the waiting car.

That was that.

It really was over, in every way.

Chapter Eighteen

For Cade, the month that followed Piper's departure passed in a blur. Things quickly settled back into their usual, peaceful routine at the ranch, as though nothing out of the ordinary had ever happened there at all. As always, there was work to be done, a million things—big and little—that needed his attention. He did them all, doing his best to lose himself in them to avoid thinking about other things.

It didn't work.

Mostly he thought about her.

How she was doing. What she was doing.

What she looked like when she smiled.

It was crazy. Caitlin hadn't dogged his thoughts this much after she'd left, and they'd been married.

One thing was the same though. He didn't hear from her, just as he hadn't heard from Caitlin beyond the divorce papers. He figured she was busy, tending to both of her sisters, dealing with her everyday life the same way he was.

He should have asked her to stay.

It was a foolish thought. He'd known her for two days. She would have thought he was crazy and probably run away as fast as she could.

Tara hadn't thought so, he acknowledged, the moments when he'd said goodbye to the girl sticking with him.

"I know you like her," she'd said, leaning close and staring him straight in the eye with a look that was far older than her years. "You're going to have to say something, because she won't."

"We've only known each other for two days," he'd said roughly, the words coming out before he could think about them. "Why would I say something?"

To this day he wondered if Tara had told Piper what he'd said. It would certainly explain why she hadn't been in touch, as if he hadn't given her reason enough to her face.

He didn't think she would have though, because the look Tara had given him just before she'd shaken her head and walked away had been too much like pity. And he'd heard her mutter under her breath, "You two deserve each other."

The hell of it was, he'd almost done it. The words had been there in those last moments before Piper left, when he'd been looking into her beautiful face, those big brown eyes, and known more than anything that he hadn't wanted her to go.

He hadn't been able to bring himself to say them, that old self-preservation instinct holding him back.

And then she was gone.

The knowledge, crazy as it was, nagged at him, unshakable, like a thorn in his side.

He should have asked her to stay.

It was Matt who finally knocked him out of his brooding, appearing in the door of his office one day. "We need to talk," he said without preamble.

Cade didn't even bother to look up. "Not now."

"Yes, now."

"If you want to keep your job, you'll back off and leave me alone right now."

"I don't want to keep my job, and neither do most of the people here. That's the problem."

Cade's head snapped up, the words managing to pierce through his irritation. "What are you talking about?"

Matt glared at him, his closed lips twitching, his mouth moving as though he was tasting something particularly bad. Finally, he sighed. "You need to go after her."

Cade just stared at him, the words not making a bit of sense. "What are you talking about?" he repeated.

Matt sighed again. "Piper," he said slowly. "Go after her."

If anything, the statement made even less sense. Cade shook his head. "*You* want me to go after her?"

"I want you to stop being a pain. You've been hell to be around this past month. You need to deal with this before we kill you."

"You can try," he muttered.

"Believe me, there's enough of us to get the job done. Even Sharon will get in on the action."

Cade threw up his hands, wanting this conversation to be over. Wanting to think about anything else.

Wanting to see her again.

At the last, he sighed, his shoulders slumping.

Damn.

He shook his head. "I'm not going to chase after a woman who doesn't want me," he said, as much to himself as to Matt.

"How do you know she doesn't want you? Have you talked to her?"

"No. She hasn't called."

"Have you called her?"

He scowled. "No," he admitted.

"So do it. Or go see her. Or something. You can't go on like this. None of us can take you going on like this."

Cade was quiet for a long moment, the question that had been dogging him, the question that had kept him from calling or doing anything to see her again, plaguing him. "What if she's not interested?" he said roughly.

Matt's expression softened the slightest bit. "Then you'll know," he said, not without a little sympathy. "You can start to get over it already."

"She doesn't belong here." Except she had. She may be a city woman, but she had fit here, in a way Caitlin never had. The house had never felt more empty than since she'd left.

"She did just fine for herself," Matt noted.

"She may not be worth the trouble." Even as he said the words, he wanted to deny them. Piper was worth the trouble. He knew it.

Matt didn't say anything for a few seconds. Then, finally, with clear reluctance, he said, "She's not Caitlin. She's one of the good ones."

Cade's eyebrows went sky-high. Coming

from Matt that was the equivalent of nominating her for sainthood. It wasn't just Caitlin he was usually sour on, it was most women and relationships, which was why this whole conversation was so bizarre.

Not for the first time, Cade couldn't help but wonder what had made Matt so jaded about women. His gut told him there was a story there. But Matt had never said and Cade hadn't asked. It wasn't the kind of thing they talked about.

"Go after her," Matt said. "You're a fool if you don't." He turned to leave. "And pretty soon a dead fool," he added over his shoulder. Then he was gone.

In the wake of Matt's departure, Cade sat in silence, doing nothing but thinking about his friend's words. About taking that chance.

About Piper.

It was a stupid idea. He sure as hell wasn't going to do it.

Two hours later he found himself in his truck, tearing down the highway toward Albuquerque to catch a flight.

He still didn't know quite what he was doing. He only knew that he was doing it, had to do it.

He couldn't call her. He didn't even know her number, though he could probably get it somehow. But he had no idea what he'd say to her on the phone, no idea what to say at all really. Maybe if he saw her, then he'd know.

And more than anything he wanted to see her.

He didn't know what would happen after that. Right now he really didn't care. That would be enough, just to see her.

He was approaching the same stretch of highway where they'd first met, he realized. The rental car had been towed long ago, of course, when the rental company had brought her a new one. The roadway was as empty as it usually was.

Even as he thought it, he caught a glimmer of something in the distance. The glimmer gradually took shape, a small, hazy form that slowly grew larger.

It was a car, he registered, approaching in the opposite lane.

He didn't think much of it—more than enough on his mind to concern himself with just another driver on the road.

But as their vehicles came near, then passed each other, he caught a quick glimpse of the car's driver out of the corner of his eye.

A woman. Shoulder-length black hair ruffling in the wind coming through the open window.

He slammed on the brakes without thinking, his heart pounding, his eyes flying to the rearview mirror to see the car that had already flown by.

It couldn't be. He had to be seeing things.

He watched as the car's brake lights came on and the vehicle screeched to a stop the same way his had. And he knew.

It wasn't possible. It couldn't be happening.

But it was.

It was her.

THIS CAN'T BE HAPPENING.

Not here, not now. She wasn't ready. This wasn't anything like she'd imagined it.

And Piper had imagined it. For one painfully long month, it seemed as though she'd done nothing else.

There had been other things to do, of course. Pam had come out of the coma three days after she and Tara had returned to Dallas. It had seemed like a definite miracle. One minute she'd still been unconscious, the next she'd been awake, with no evident long-term effects from what she'd been through.

Pam remembered exactly what had happened to her and had confirmed everything they'd uncovered about Tara's kidnapping, Larson and Castillo. Piper had explained everything to her before the FBI was informed she was awake and anyone came to talk to her.

She and Pam had spoken more in the past month than they had in the last ten years. It was like finding a piece of herself she'd lost. Piper wanted to get to know her sister again, and wanted her sisters to know each other. It already felt as if they'd made great strides to doing just that.

Then Pam was ready to resume her life and Tara had returned to school, and Piper had gone back home to Boston.

But the entire time Cade had never been far from her thoughts. Lying in bed at night, when she was finally alone and her time was entirely her own, she'd thought of him, and imagined what it would be like to see him again. Imagined if he had suddenly appeared in Dallas to check on Pam, to check on *her*. Imagined if she had arrived home in Boston and he'd been there on her doorstep, waiting for her, wanting to see her.

They were foolish fantasies. The man hadn't asked her to stay or come back, hadn't offered the slightest personal gesture when they'd parted ways. There was no way that would ever happen.

But the fantasies hadn't faded, and finally she couldn't do it anymore. Couldn't spend her nights dreaming about him, her days picturing him, wondering what he was up to. She'd thought what had happened when she'd left had been an ending, closure, but it wasn't. No, he hadn't said anything, but she hadn't, either, no matter how badly she'd wanted to. And since she hadn't, there was still a chance....

Whatever happened, she needed to know. Needed to see him again, if only one more time.

Never had she imagined it happening like this.

But it was.

She should have called, but she hadn't known what to say. Finally it had seemed easier just to come. She'd thought she'd figure out what to say by the time she got here.

She still didn't have a clue.

A wave of doubts suddenly washed over her. What would this look like? Would it seem desperate? The questions she'd been holding back from the moment she'd decided to come here broke free. Who did something like this? Who came all the way across the country with no warning to see a man she'd known for two days?

Finally certainty settled over her, and she knew she didn't care about any of that. Not how it might look. Not how she might come across. The hell with it.

She wanted her chance.

She watched in the rearview mirror as the driver's door opened, and that long, tall figure she knew so well, the one that had haunted her dreams, stepped out of the truck and onto the pavement. He turned toward her car and stood there, lit from behind by the sun, facing her. Waiting.

Like it or not, this was happening. She couldn't sit there forever. Nor did she want to. She may not be ready, but this was why she'd come all this way. To see him again.

She sucked in a breath, then reached for the door handle, her hand shaking.

He was standing beside his truck, hands buried in his pockets. Her heart hitched at the sight of him. She'd tried to tell herself that she'd romanticized her image of him over the past month, that he wasn't really as big, as broad shouldered, as rugged and masculine and beautiful as she remembered him. And he wasn't.

He looked even better.

She walked toward him slowly, drinking in the sight of him. Any fear that she wouldn't feel the same spark vanished as she felt it stronger than ever, along with the nervousness that was brand-new but just as potent. She peered closely at his face for the slightest hint of what he was thinking, but of course his expression remained as stoic and unreadable as ever.

Then they were face-to-face, just a few feet from one another.

"Hi," she said, the word so breathless it was barely audible.

"Hi," he said roughly. "What are you doing here?"

The words were neither as welcoming as she would have hoped nor as cold as she might have feared. "I came to see you."

He was silent for a beat. "Why?"

"I thought you might want to know how everything turned out, and I wanted to thank you again and see how you were doing...." She trailed off, the words failing to come.

"You could have called," he pointed out.

"I know. I just...I just wanted to see you." She swallowed hard, terror climbing in her throat at the admission she was about to make, every instinct within her wanting to hold the words back. She couldn't do it. She couldn't put herself out there. She couldn't risk so very much. Her pride. Her heart.

She had to.

She took a steadying breath and just let the words come out.

"I missed you."

The words hung there in the air between them. She waited, breathless, to see what he would say, how he would react.

He didn't, not really. His expression shifted slightly, enough that he looked surprised, though she couldn't tell if it was pleasantly or not. His mouth worked, but nothing came out, as though he couldn't find the words.

It wasn't the reaction she'd needed. In fact, it was exactly what she'd feared. She'd embarrassed herself, embarrassed them both, and now he didn't know what to say.

Humiliation washing over her, she couldn't take the silence anymore. She glanced away, spotting his truck. She realized he'd been driving away from the ranch. If she hadn't recognized the truck, or he hadn't stopped... Well, then they wouldn't be having this incredibly awkward moment. "I guess I came at just the right time or I really would have missed you." She blinked. "Oh, you were going somewhere. Were you going somewhere important?"

"Yeah."

"Oh. Okay." She did her best to choke back

her disappointment. Apparently this reunion was going to be shorter than she'd imagined, though based on how it was going, that was probably a good thing. He probably needed to be on his way. What could she do, hang around the ranch until he came back? She worked to keep her tone light and her emotions from showing. "Where were you going?"

"To the airport." He swallowed, and when he spoke again, it was softly, his voice rough. "I was going to see you."

It was the last thing she ever would have expected him to say. The sound of those words coming from him, in that voice, were better than any fantasy she'd conjured. Because this was real. She knew how hard it had been for him to admit it, as much as it had been for her.

"Really?" she breathed.

"Yeah." He swallowed, his face more vulnerable and naked than she'd ever seen it. "I missed you, too."

The words were as sincere and straightforward as anything he'd ever said to her, and she knew he was telling the truth. The backs of her eyes began to burn, with relief, with joy.

And then he was moving forward so fast, as though released from the restraints that had been holding him back, she barely had time to process it. One moment he was standing so very far from her, the next his arms were around her, crushing her to him, holding her tight.

She clung to him just as tightly. This was everything she'd dreamed of for the last month, the longest of her life. She felt his heart pounding in time with hers, breathed in the scent of him, absorbed the feeling of his body pressed against hers. She tried to imprint it all on her memory, never wanting to forget this moment.

Finally she pushed back against his chest, needing to see his face. He eased his hold, but didn't let her go. God knew, she didn't want him to. Not entirely. She lifted her hands to his face, that beautiful face she'd seen in her dreams, so much better in person. "I can't believe we almost missed each other." In more ways than one.

"I should have called," he said ruefully.

"So should I," she admitted. The absurdness of it hit her hard, and a giddy laugh burst from her throat. "Neither of us is very good at this, are we?"

He grinned, the sight so beautiful she almost couldn't stand it. "No. Guess we'll have to work on that."

"Yes, we will." They had a lot to work out, and she didn't have the slightest doubt in the world they would. Nothing could possibly be as hard as this had been. They were past the worst.

She finally realized where they were, standing in the middle of the highway with the vehicles blocking the road. "We should probably get out of here before someone comes along."

"Yeah, we have better things to do than stand here," he said, the words sending a thrill up her spine.

"Guess we can't abandon my car along the side of the road this time. Should I follow you back or do you want to follow me since my car's already headed in that direction?"

He just looked at her, that beautiful grin on his face, before shrugging. "Does it matter?"

It didn't, she acknowledged, joy soaring through her in the face of his smile. The only thing that did was that they were going to the same place.

And they were. Back to the Triple C.

Back home.

Together.

* * * * *

LARGER-PRINT BOOKS!
GET 2 FREE LARGER-PRINT NOVELS PLUS
2 FREE GIFTS!

&Harlequin®

INTRIGUE

BREATHTAKING ROMANTIC SUSPENSE

YES! Please send me 2 FREE LARGER-PRINT Harlequin Intrigue® novels and my 2 FREE gifts (gifts are worth about $10). After receiving them, if I don't wish to receive any more books, I can return the shipping statement marked "cancel." If I don't cancel, I will receive 6 brand-new novels every month and be billed just $5.24 per book in the U.S. or $5.99 per book in Canada. That's a saving of at least 13% off the cover price! It's quite a bargain! Shipping and handling is just 50¢ per book in the U.S. and 75¢ per book in Canada.* I understand that accepting the 2 free books and gifts places me under no obligation to buy anything. I can always return a shipment and cancel at any time. Even if I never buy another book, the two free books and gifts are mine to keep forever.

199/399 HDN FERE

Name	(PLEASE PRINT)

Address	Apt. #

City	State/Prov.	Zip/Postal Code

Signature (if under 18, a parent or guardian must sign)

Mail to the **Reader Service:**
IN U.S.A.: P.O. Box 1867, Buffalo, NY 14240-1867
IN CANADA: P.O. Box 609, Fort Erie, Ontario L2A 5X3

Not valid for current subscribers to Harlequin Intrigue Larger-Print books.

**Are you a subscriber to Harlequin Intrigue books
and want to receive the larger-print edition?
Call 1-800-873-8635 today or visit www.ReaderService.com.**

* Terms and prices subject to change without notice. Prices do not include applicable taxes. Sales tax applicable in N.Y. Canadian residents will be charged applicable taxes. Offer not valid in Quebec. This offer is limited to one order per household. All orders subject to credit approval. Credit or debit balances in a customer's account(s) may be offset by any other outstanding balance owed by or to the customer. Please allow 4 to 6 weeks for delivery. Offer available while quantities last.

Your Privacy—The Reader Service is committed to protecting your privacy. Our Privacy Policy is available online at www.ReaderService.com or upon request from the Reader Service.

We make a portion of our mailing list available to reputable third parties that offer products we believe may interest you. If you prefer that we not exchange your name with third parties, or if you wish to clarify or modify your communication preferences, please visit us at www.ReaderService.com/consumerschoice or write to us at Reader Service Preference Service, P.O. Box 9062, Buffalo, NY 14269. Include your complete name and address.

HILP11B

He jabbed a finger in Larson's face. "You.